She looked down into her baby's face.

He was real, this small person who had been strangely unreal all these months. Now he was here in person. A part of her, yet something very much apart. He had taken his place in the universe. She took one of his tiny hands, examining each finger, one by one. She was in awe. He stirred, made little mewing sounds. He was so warm, precious. Someday, most assuredly, he would grow up to tower over her with long legs, broad shoulders. But now he lay in her arms, belonging completely to her. She would treasure this moment, cherish it, keep it in her heart forever.

"We're going to be all right, Danny boy," she whispered. "You and me, we're going to do just fine. I promise."

JANE PEART

CIRCLE OF LOVE

Love Inspired®

Published by Steeple Hill Books™

STEEPLE HILL BOOKS

Steeple
Hill™

ISBN 0-373-87093-0

CIRCLE OF LOVE

Visit us at www.steeplehill.com

Printed in U.S.A.

Award-winning and bestselling author
Jane Peart grew up in North Carolina and
was educated in New England. Jane and her
husband now reside in Northern California,
which is often a setting for her novels.

In more than twenty books which include her
bestselling Orphan Train West series, Jane has
brought to readers the timeless themes of
family, faith and committed love.

PART I

Chapter One

Her hand on the doorknob, Elyn Ross stood for a moment looking back at her apartment. Stripped now of all the personal touches, it looked almost the same as the day she had rented it. Fresh out of art school, three weeks into a new job, she had been so excited. Then, her future had seemed to have so many possibilities, held so much promise. That was before anything had happened....

She remained standing there, remembering. Then, because she was afraid she might change her mind, she quickly shut the door and turned the key in the lock. She ran down the outside stairs, out to the parking lot where her car was packed and waiting. She tossed her handbag and tote into the back seat, got in the car and without a backward glance headed out of the city.

There was little traffic this early Sunday morning. Mist beaded her windshield and she turned on the wipers. By the time she reached the Golden Gate Bridge, curls of gray fog swirled around the lower girders, obscuring the railings and the bay below. At the sight of this familiar landmark Elyn felt a pang of regret. Her rush to get away had not allowed time to feel any sadness about leaving the city she had come to love. San Francisco was the place that had once held all her dreams of making it in the art world. Now she was leaving not because she wanted to, but to save herself, to save her soul....

For the past three days she had been functioning on automatic, doing what needed to be done. After all the tears, the hurt, a deadly calm had come over her. She had felt strangely numb. Now that sensation was wearing off. In its place a heart-wrenching pain had come. Would it ever go away?

She turned on the radio. Immediately the interior of the small car was filled with Michael Crawford's voice singing ''Music of the Night.'' Elyn snapped it off quickly. *The Phantom of the Opera* had been one of the first outings she'd had with Dex. Somehow he had managed to get those hard-to-find tickets to the Broadway musical, tenth row center. It had been a night of magic, of glamour. Elyn had been thrilled by a glimpse of the kind of life lived by people like Dex.

No wonder she had been dazzled. Wouldn't any small-town girl from the Midwest have been? The elegant restaurants, the openings, the galas, the parties in Hillsboro at mansions owned by people in the social circles in which he moved. Weekends in Carmel, ski lodges at Squaw Valley, sailing on the Bay. It had been a breathless whirl of new experiences. No wonder her head had spun.

Elyn's hands tightened on the steering wheel. She had been swept up in it all, trusted the pledges, the promises, the fairy-tale ending....

That it should end like this was unreal. She shuddered, reliving their terrible quarrel.

Dex had been angrier than she had ever seen him. His temper had erupted savagely, leaving her shaken and speechless. Devastated, she had run from his fury.

During the sleepless night that followed, Elyn came to terms with what had happened. The morning after, flowers arrived with an envelope enclosing a check that she tore into little pieces. A gesture that symbolized all her torn hopes. Instinctively, she knew there was no going back. Too much had been said, too much revealed. Whatever they'd had was gone.

All through that day she moved as if in a trance. She went to the bank, drew out all her money from checking and closed her savings account. When she got back to her apartment, the light on the answering machine was flashing, signaling a call. She pushed the Play button and listened. Dex's voice was cool, controlled, yet underneath Elyn could still detect the anger.

"I'm flying to L.A. this afternoon. I'll be at the Beverly Hilton. You can reach me there." There was a pause. "I'll be in meetings most of the day, but you can call after seven." Another pause. "Be sensible, Elyn."

Be sensible? That was what she was doing. She would

leave the city. Burn all her bridges behind her. Since Dex had never let her pay for anything, she had enough money to last for a while, until…until what? She wasn't sure.

Dex's words from the other night still rang in her ears. "You knew this wasn't in the game plan." Of course, she knew that. Neither had *this* been in hers. But his solution was out of the question. She pressed the Erase button, wiping out the message. Why would she call him? There was nothing else to say. She knew him well enough to think he would change.

What she was doing was right. To leave now, without any more ugly scenes, recriminations. Dex had made his position clear. And it was unacceptable to her. If she did not comply with his demand; they had no future. There was nothing more to discuss; any hope of reconciliation had been irrevocably shattered.

In a way it was ironic. Dex had taught her a lot of things. For example, how to end things. She had seen Dex end things before—a friendship, a business, a nonprofitable investment. He never looked back, never second-guessed himself, never seemed to have regrets. When something was over, it was over. He moved on. Well, now she was moving on. Leaving without saying where she'd gone. Leaving no clues so there would be no way to trace her—although she doubted he would try.

It was herself she didn't trust. If she stayed in the city, was she strong enough to carry through this alternative plan? Safe from his power to persuade? Dex had to be in control. If he couldn't be, he bullied. That was why it was best to remove herself. Put it all behind her. Forget him.

But, of course, that was impossible. No matter what, she could not completely forget what would forever link them. She was carrying his child.

Chapter Two

Elyn bypassed Marin, kept driving north, not knowing exactly where she was heading, not caring. The freeway without its usual traffic stretched ahead into infinity. She had driven an hour, maybe two, when she suddenly began to feel tired. The emotional stress of the past three days had taken its toll. Her neck felt stiff, her shoulders ached. She should probably stop soon, rest. On impulse, she took the next exit ramp marked Napa.

From the freeway she turned onto a two-lane highway. It wove between wooded groves of poplars and manzanita. On either side were hillsides where sheep roamed, fenced pastures with cows, meadows where horses frolicked. Set back from the road were Victorian houses shaded by gnarled oak trees, surrounded by vineyards. How charming and peaceful. It seemed a million miles from San Francisco. She had left that city under gray clouds and fog, yet here, even in late March, spring seemed to have arrived. She passed orchards of fruit trees beginning to bud and a delicate green softened the branches of other trees.

She slowed at a crossroads, read the sign Calistoga 17 miles, and continued in that direction.

As she drove along the winding road, she was surprised to see several multicolored hot-air balloons drifting in the cloudless, blue sky. She felt a small stirring of hope in her heart. Maybe they were a sign that no matter what, she could find a way to go on.

Only a short distance from the pastoral scene she was in the center of town. At the traffic light she turned onto the main street, lined on both sides with a variety of stores. Restaurants, art galleries and specialty stores of all kinds. Signs offered the healthful benefits of many available hot springs spas. Elyn remembered hearing about the famous mineral springs in this part of California's wine country.

This might be a great place to take her time out. A place to get her head together, to curl up for a while and begin the process of healing, to try to decide what to do next....

She took two cruises through the downtown section, then drove slowly onto some of the other tree-lined streets, looking for somewhere to stay. She noticed a Vacancy sign at a pink-and-white Victorian bed-and-breakfast and pulled into the parking area. It looked secluded, yet welcoming.

Within a few minutes she found herself being shown a pretty room wallpapered in trellised roses, a four-poster bed piled with lacy pillows and French doors opening onto a sun-drenched patio. A path lined with oleander bushes led to the swimming pool from which she could hear the voices of other guests and the splash of water.

Quickly Elyn changed into her swimsuit and went out to one of the lounge chairs and stretched out. The sun on her face and arms felt lovely. Gradually some of her weariness and tension began to leave. She flexed her arms and arched her toes. Maybe she would take advantage of a full treatment outlined in the brochure she'd been given when she checked in: mud bath, Jacuzzi, herbal wrap, massage… Under her sunglasses, she closed her eyes. It seemed almost possible to forget what had happened, why she was here.

Reality soon penetrated the shell of denial in which she had wrapped herself for the past few days. She was going to have to make some decisions about the future.

Suddenly she felt terribly alone, filled with panic. She had to tell someone, to get some support.

The sun had long since moved beyond the treetops. Unable to relax any longer, Elyn went inside, got dressed. As she buttoned the denim skirt around her slender waist, she caught her reflection in the dressing table mirror. How much longer before she began to show? Unconsciously, her hands smoothed her flat midriff and tummy. A baby? Was it possible? Could it be real? Was this actually happening to *her?*

Elyn stared at the image looking back at her.

Where was the girl of six months ago? Even six weeks

ago? The girl with the layered hairstyle with its sunny highlights? The girl with the happy smile, the shining brown eyes?

Someone had replaced her. The eyes were now filled with fear; the mouth Dex had loved to kiss drooped at the corners.

She suppressed a shudder and turned away from the reflection that mocked her. She pulled on a bouclé knit sweater, grabbed her leather shoulder bag and went out along the flower-bordered path to the street. There she paused briefly, glancing in both directions. She saw a phone booth at the corner and walked toward it.

She dug in her handbag for her wallet, drew out her phone card. Her hand shook a little as she dialed the familiar number. She held her breath as the phone rang at the other end. She could picture her grandmother frowning, annoyed at having one of her favorite programs interrupted. Possibly a rerun of *The Waltons*. Then with a sigh she would turn down the TV and make her way from the living room into the hall.

The phone had always been placed in the hall at her grandparents' home. No concessions made to convenience. No wall phone in the kitchen, nor one by the bedside. As a teenager living with them, Elyn had resented that lack of privacy. Someone was always within earshot of her conversation.

As she waited for the phone to be picked up, she felt nervous perspiration bead her upper lip and forehead.

She slid the phone booth's door open a crack to take a long breath. Then she heard her grandmother's voice.

"Hello."

"Grandma, it's Elyn." Her throat was tight.

"Why, Elyn, this is a surprise." Grandma's voice had that tinge of reproach Elyn recognized at once. Grandma could always inject guilt by using that tone. Elyn knew she deserved it. She hadn't written regularly or called, especially since being involved with Dex. There was so much she couldn't tell her grandmother that she had avoided writing or phoning.

Now, however, she felt the desperate need to connect with what her life had been before—before San Francisco, before Dex....

"How's work?" Grandma asked.

It seemed a logical question, but totally irrelevant now. If she explained she had quit her job at the ad agency by E-mail, no notice, no references requested, her grandmother would chide her for being irresponsible. The explanation of why was the hard part.

Why make up nonsense? Elyn swallowed, then stammering a little said, "Grandma I—I'd like to come home for a while."

There was a slight pause followed by a reserved, "That would be nice, dear. When were you thinking of coming?"

"Soon," Elyn answered, sensing some lack of spontaneity in her grandmother's response, hesitant to add, "As soon as possible, please."

"And how long were you planning to stay?"

This was a question Elyn had not expected.

"The reason I'm asking, dear, is that your grandfather and I were thinking about joining a group for a bus tour to Virginia, visiting some of the historic spots and ending up in Washington D.C., in time to see the cherry blossoms in bloom."

Elyn felt her knees sag a little. Of course, she should have considered the possibility that her grandparents might have plans of their own. They were active in Middlefield senior circles. Even back when she was in high school they'd had a busy social life. Everything was scheduled, marked precisely on the calendar that hung next to the gleaming refrigerator in Grandma's immaculate kitchen. Elyn shut her eyes, seeing the starched café curtains at the windows, the matching canisters lined up on the Formica counters, the quilted potholders above the stove. Everything neat, in order. Nothing out of place.

Elyn heard Grandma's voice, but it became muffled, almost drowned out by the loud beating of her own heart. There was a pause on the line and she realized she hadn't been really listening. She knew she was coming unglued, but she couldn't seem to help it. Tears streamed unchecked down her cheeks.

"So when we know the dates, we can let you know," Grandma said. Another pause. "Elyn?"

Elyn swallowed, trying to form the words over the hard lump rising in her throat. Then she just blurted out,

"Grandma, the reason I called is…I'm pregnant. May I come stay with you and Grampa?"

The silence that followed was electric. Elyn could almost hear the line crackle. Even before Grandma spoke again, Elyn knew it had been a mistake to call, to ask, to even *think* of going there.

Grandma's voice was shaky. "I hardly know what to say, Elyn. I'm deeply shocked, of course. But then you knew I would be." Silence stretched agonizingly. Then, "I certainly don't…can't—I mean, there's no use my asking how this happened.…" She broke off. "I don't know what to say."

Elyn squeezed her eyes tight, imagining the older woman's face, its smooth pink surface crumpled with distress. Beyond her grandmother's small, plump figure standing in the hall, clutching the phone, Elyn could see into the living room; saw her grandfather sitting in his recliner, reading, beside his chair, the magazine rack holding neatly arranged issues of *National Geographic* and *Reader's Digest*. He was very deaf now, unable to hear the conversation taking place only a few feet from where he sat. Content, his pleasant face bland, he was undisturbed by the drama taking place only a heartbeat away.

Elyn choked back sobs. She should have known better than to expect understanding, even sympathy. It had been wrong to ask for refuge. How could she have possibly thought she could just barge into the placid routine of her grandparents' lives?

Her grandmother's next words summed up all that she should have known. "There's no point saying I'm deeply disappointed in you, Elyn. You're over twenty-one and should have known better. All that is useless now. But your coming here—well, I hardly think that would be a good idea. This is a small town. People don't have the liberal views they *evidently* have in *California*. I don't think it would do at all."

Elyn nodded wordlessly as her grandmother's voice regained its firmness.

"Besides, your grandfather hasn't been at all well lately...hasn't even been to Kiwanis the last two months. I don't know what he'll think when I tell him—no, Elyn, I'm sorry, but your coming here is out of the question."

She could see Grandma shaking her perfectly styled head as she spoke.

Elyn could not think of any reply. It was the response she should have foreseen. If she had been thinking rationally.

"There must be places out there you could go...." Grandma ventured, and Elyn's fingers tightened on the phone. Of course, that would be Grandma's suggestion, find some institution for unwed mothers. The Middlefield solution. "Visiting a relative in Iowa" used to be the euphemism for a girl in trouble disappearing for a few months.

Elyn didn't remember much of the rest of the conversation. She just remembered murmuring something about being sorry before hanging up. Slowly she replaced the phone on the hook. She regretted the impulse to call her grandmother. She had only managed to upset her. And for what? What could Grandma do?

Elyn didn't blame her. She was right. Middlefield was a small town. To expose her grandparents to the rampant gossip that would ensue if their pregnant, unmarried granddaughter came there—especially one whom they had raised after her parents died—would be a terrible blow to their pride. Their spotless reputation would be ruined by the prodigal's return.

Elyn understood. It was unfair to expect any other reaction. Still, she needed someone to confide in. A sounding board, a bridge until she got her bearings. She felt so rootless, so overwhelmed. She thought of her Aunt Pat. She wasn't a real aunt, but her father's cousin whom she had always called aunt. Pat was different from the other women in a family of devoted wives and dedicated mothers. She was the one everyone referred to as a career woman. She had started out as a mail clerk in the local bank, risen to become a teller and eventually a loan officer in St. Louis. Elyn had always admired her independence, self-assurance and success. Surely, Aunt Pat would be nonjudgmental. Perhaps she would let her come and stay for a while at her city apartment until… Well, until Elyn could think straight, make some plans. Yes, she would get some good commonsense advice from Aunt Pat.

She checked the phone number in her pocket address book, then dialed Pat's number. A few minutes later,

Elyn realized this, too, had been a mistake. Aunt Pat registered shock, but not in the same way as Grandma, nor for the same reasons.

"I can't believe you were so stupid. That two adults in this day and age would be so careless!" she gasped. "Not to take any precautions is simply irresponsible and crazy. I cannot believe it. Certainly, you knew better."

No argument there, Elyn echoed mentally. But what good was thinking or saying that now? It didn't help anything. And Pat wasn't interested in helping. She offered neither advice nor support. She did offer money but Elyn said no thanks, she was fine.

Wearily she hung up the receiver, opened the door of the phone booth and stepped out into the quiet, dark night. She was deadly calm. She had been desolate, desperate to make those calls. Yet maybe she'd had to do it. To face the reality. No one was going to rescue her. Elyn straightened her shoulders and walked back to the B-and-B. Whatever lay ahead for her was her problem. No one else's.

Chapter Three

Elyn woke up the next morning in a sun-filled room. For a minute she felt disoriented. Where was she? Then slowly yesterday came back into her mind. Yesterday and the day before, and the one before that, and the night of the quarrel. She closed her eyes again, wishing she could blot out the memory. She wished she could just pull the sheet over her head and slip back into the oblivion of sleep.

But there was today to be faced. And the day after that and so on and on for the rest of her life. Firmly, she repeated the old adage: One day at a time.

As she got out of bed, a wave of dizziness swept over her and she sat down quickly. Probably lack of food. After making the phone calls last evening, she had not had the appetite to eat dinner. Instead she had gone right to bed. Then came a jolt of reality. Of course. It had to be early pregnancy queasiness. The dizziness soon passed, but, she was left sober and thoughtful.

Elyn grabbed the B-and-B brochure off the nightstand. It stated that a buffet breakfast was served to guests on the screened porch. She decided to take advantage of it and got dressed. She was feeling fine again and hungry.

The porch was shaded by a wisteria vine and furnished with white wicker. On a long table a picture-perfect buffet was set out—large pitcher of orange juice, a platter of luscious-looking fruit, an assortment of yogurts, a bowl of granola, two kinds of muffins, a variety of teas and a coffeemaker. Two couples who were helping themselves to the feast nodded and said good morning. Then they took their plates to small tables for two at the other end of the porch. Elyn's gaze followed them.

Couples. This B-and-B was the ideal place for couples to come on a romantic weekend and to enjoy that mineral springs. It was the sort of place Dex would write off as "too quaint, a bit too much charm." But she liked it. She would have to stop evaluating things through Dex's sometimes cynical view. She also had to get used to the idea that she was no longer part of a couple.

As she settled herself at a table and sipped her coffee, she read more of the brochure. There was a great deal about the "Mustard Festival" described in the colorful pamphlet inserted into the brochure. It was a celebration of the food, wine, art, agriculture and history of Napa Valley. Many exciting events were planned during the special season. Included in the brochure was a map of the town showing the locations of shops, galleries, restaurants, a museum and other attractions. After she finished eating, she decided she would look around. She was in no hurry. After all, she had nowhere to be, no place to go, no one waiting for her.

It was a lovely day, perfect for a stroll along the sidewalks in the center of town. Stores were just opening, people greeting each other, some carrying containers of coffee and bakery bags on their way to work. Everything had an appealing casualness in direct contrast to the frenetic San Francisco downtown. People in sport clothes were buying morning papers, then heading for one of the many restaurants open for breakfast. This was a tourist Mecca for sure. It lacked the blatant tourism of other California resorts and yet everywhere were reminders that it catered to the visitor. Signs extolling the many health and relaxation benefits of various accommodations were discreetly displayed. Along each side of the main street there were restaurants offering all kinds of culinary specialties, as well as spas, wineries and tasting rooms, shops, galleries, antiques, ice cream, stationery and collectible stores. Again, Elyn could not help noticing couples. Were the young ones honeymooners? The older ones celebrating anniversaries? Or simply sans children learning to be just a couple again?

An older couple directly in front of her, arms entwined, stopped to gaze at a window display in one of the gift shops, then turned to each other and kissed and hugged. It was so natural, it was not at all offensive, yet it struck Elyn like a blow. Seeing their show of affection made the painful memory of being in love and its loss sharp.

A sense of her own vulnerability surfaced. It was as piercing as when she had been a ten-year-old growing up without parents.

All her life Elyn had longed for safety and security, a sense of belonging, being loved for herself, cared for, protected. She had hoped to find that with Dex. A false hope as it turned out.

Elyn dragged herself back from vain regrets. She would have to get used to seeing other people happy or— or what? Become bitter, envious, depressed?

As she reached the end of one side of the main street, she saw a black wrought iron gate over which was the name The Crow's Nest. A brick walkway led back to the side entrance of a large Victorian house. A sign on the red-painted door said: Welcome. Come in to Browse or Buy, or Just Enjoy.

Inside smelled heavenly, a mixture of potpourri, scented candles and perfumed soaps.

"May I help you? Or do you just want to browse around and not be bothered?" a lilting voice asked. Startled, Elyn turned to see a young woman with quantities of flaming-red hair perched behind a counter cluttered with wicker baskets spilling out varicolored chiffon scarves. She had not been aware of the woman until she'd spoken.

At first glance the woman reminded Elyn of a combination of Fergie and Wynona Judd. She was old-fashioned candy-box pretty. Even features, fresh complexion, startlingly blue eyes, a sweetly curved mouth that when she smiled showed deep dimples.

"I'm Veronica Bailey, the resident crow!" She laughed, pointing to the sign at the door. "The name of the shop—Crow's Nest—that's me. You know how crows are always taking bits and pieces of everything and putting it in their nests? Well, this is what this place is and why the name. I started it out as a vintage clothing shop, but I kept finding things I adored. When my own apartment got too full, I started bringing things down here and people kept buying them and asking for this and that and so I kept going to estate sales and garage sales and flea markets and—" she flung out both hands, wiggling bejeweled fingers with red-lacquered nails "—voilà!"

"It's wonderful. I love it," Elyn told her, looking around. "I don't know where to begin."

The shop was filled with irresistible things, all presented in such attractive ways. There were flower arrangements, baskets, quaint dolls and stuffed animals handmade out of calico, checkered and flowered fabrics and other eye-catching collectibles. There was also an annex with racks of antique clothes. Several dressmaker forms were clothed in the Gibson Girl style—tucked and embroidered lace-trimmed blouses stood alongside forms flaunting flapper era sheaths, sequined, accordion pleated and fringed, with accessories of velvet evening opera capes, Spanish shawls and satin dance slippers with jeweled buckles.

"It's simply magical," Elyn told the owner as she emerged through the door made of strings of glittering glass beads.

"Are you looking for a special gift for someone or something for yourself? Your house or your spouse?" the woman asked. Huge green plastic earrings swung wildly as she tilted her head inquiringly.

"Actually, nothing and no one," Elyn told her. "I'm just passing through and decided to stop. I've been wandering around town this morning. I was intrigued by your shop's name so I came in. It's like walking into some fantasy grandmother's attic, isn't it?"

"I like that. No one ever put it quite that way. You must be a writer?"

"Not really. I did work for an advertising agency, wrote copy. I'm more an artist."

"An artist? Oh, this must be my lucky day. Or do you believe in serendipity or synchronicity or anything like that? I need a new logo, for business cards, to use when I send out notices for sales, that sort of thing. Could you design something like that?"

"Well, yes, of course. But I don't know how long I'm going to be here. As I said, I'm just passing through—"

"Where are you headed?"

"Actually..." Elyn hesitated, then replied, "Nowhere. I'm just trying to find some place I might like to live for a while."

"Are you by yourself...if that isn't being too nosy?"

"Yes...I mean...no, it isn't too nosy and I *am* by myself," Elyn answered, realizing that it was the first time in almost two years she could say that.

"Why not consider staying here? You'd love it. I came here myself a few years ago on vacation, never dreaming I'd stay, much less go into business. It really is a wonderful place, especially for a single woman."

The shopkeeper came around the counter. She wore a black long-sleeve T-shirt, an ankle-length sarong-wrap batik print skirt and clunky heeled sandals.

"I'm trying out some outfits to wear to the Mustard Festival gala. Big social deal in these parts. Showing up there is better than a full-page ad in the Valley News. Maybe even a mention in Olive Hill's column 'The Grapevine.'

"I'll tell you what. I was about to close up for lunch. Why don't we go somewhere together and talk? I'm a one-woman chamber of commerce. Maybe I can convince you this is the place you were looking for. Okay?"

"Why not?" Elyn shrugged.

"I'll just put the Closed sign on the door and we'll be off." As they walked down the brick path out to the street, she said, "By the way, my friends call me Ronnie."

When they reached the restaurant, Ronnie suggested they find an umbrellaed table on the sunny patio. Ronnie recommended the spinach quiche and ordered a Caesar salad herself.

"Watching my weight," she declared. "Which, of course, *you* would know nothing about."

"Well, I don't know for how long that will be the case," Elyn said wryly. "I should be eating for two. I'm pregnant." Once the words were out, she wondered why she had volunteered such private information. Maybe she had wanted to say it out loud to make it more real. Maybe she wanted to see Ronnie's reaction. Maybe she just had to tell someone—even a perfect stranger. Whatever the reason, it was said.

Momentarily Ronnie's eyes widened, then she smiled. "Well, good for you." She paused, then added, "So, I take it you're in this alone?"

"The father wanted nothing to do with it," Elyn answered. "I'm not saying this to gain sympathy, that's just the fact."

"Right." Ronnie nodded briskly. "All the more reason for you to stay here."

"What you said about the possibility of finding freelance art work interested me. I have to earn a living."

"I wasn't just saying that," Ronnie assured her. "There are new businesses starting up here all the time. Some don't make it, but then a lot of them do. This is a very art conscious town. It's also individualistic and open to new ideas."

"I'd always hoped to be able to make a living with my art, but I got sidetracked for a while. The man I was involved with thought it wasn't a serious goal. He considered it more or less my hobby. He didn't want it to take up too much of my time. He wanted me to be available when he wanted to go someplace, to fit into his plans.'' An edge of bitterness crept into Elyn's tone. ''But everything's different now.''

Elyn was surprised at how easily she was telling Ronnie all this. Somewhere she had read there was something therapeutic about pouring out your heart to a stranger. People did it all the time in airports, on trains, in hospital waiting rooms. She also believed nothing happened by chance. Taking the Napa turnoff from the freeway, going into The Crow's Nest this morning, meeting Veronica Bailey—it was all in some plan....

Besides, there was something so likable about Ronnie. So open and generous Elyn felt they would become friends. And she badly needed one.

Their lunch came and they ate, drank two cups of de-caffeinated coffee each and talked and talked.

''You'll need a place to live,'' Ronnie said. ''I'd say stay with me, but my apartment is worse than the shop. Not a square inch to spare. But a Realtor friend of mine is a genius at finding the right place for people. Liz Miller, just down the street. Tell her I sent you. I'm sure she'll have you settled in a jiffy.''

Throwing her diet to the wind, Ronnie ordered carrot cake for both of them. ''This is a celebration.''

After they finished lunch, Ronnie walked with Elyn back to the street and pointed her in the direction of the Realtor's office. As they stood at the corner curb, a blue pickup stopped at the crosswalk. The driver stuck his head out the cab window and waved.

''Hiya, Bird Lady!'' he called to Ronnie. His grin revealed white teeth against a tan face. "Who's minding the store?"

The printing on the truck door read General Contractor.

Before Ronnie could give the man a matching retort, the light changed and with a thumbs-up gesture he drove off.

"Doug Stevens, a really neat guy," Ronnie told Elyn. "He did some of the remodeling for my shop. Very creative. Came up with some great ideas I wouldn't have thought of for extra storage, that sort of thing."

A few minutes later they parted. "Good luck," Ronnie said, turning to go back to her shop. "Let me know how it turns out."

At the door of the Realtor's office, Elyn hesitated. Maybe this was irrational, making such a quick decision. But keeping the momentum going seemed the only way to keep from falling apart. So far, concentrating on the present kept her from dwelling on the recent past or the frightening future. If she was making a mistake, she'd find out soon enough.

She was convinced meeting Ronnie had not been just chance. And looking for a place to rent seemed the right thing to do. If there wasn't anything available at a reasonable price, then she had the option to move on. She took a long breath and turned the knob, then walked inside.

The woman she assumed was Liz Miller was on the phone when Elyn entered. She looked over the half glasses that hung from the jeweled chain around her neck

Circle of Love

and indicated Elyn should take a seat opposite her desk. When she finished her conversation, she replaced the receiver and smiled. "What can I do for you?" she asked.

Elyn introduced herself, mentioning Ronnie's name, and told the Realtor what she hoped to find.

"I think I have just the place for you," she said, flipping through her Rolodex. "It's just come on the market, actually. A cottage on the estate called Meadowmead, the Thorne family vineyards. Originally it was the overseer's home. Been empty for ages. Old Miss Thorne still lives in the main house and didn't want to rent it to just anybody. But recently it's been renovated and put up for rent. I don't know what changed her mind. Finances, maybe.

"Here it is." She pulled out a card. "Let's see. Two bedrooms, completely remodeled, modernized kitchen, bath. I know the contractor who did the work. Doug Stevens. Excellent reputation. Honest as the day's long. Great guy..."

Odd that name coming up again. Doug Stevens. But then, in a small town everyone knew everyone else. Not like San Francisco where Elyn hadn't even known the people in her apartment building.

"Yes, indeed, this should be fine for a single person." Again, the woman peered over the edge of her glasses at Elyn. "It seems several applicants were turned down by Miss Thorne. I think she's pretty particular about who she rents to, seeing as that the cottage is so close to her own house on the property. So renting it to you will need her approval."

A warning flag went up in Elyn's mind.

"The place sounds perfect," Elyn said. "But I should tell you I'm expecting a baby."

Liz Miller gave her a sharp look. "You certainly don't look it. How soon?"

"December."

"Oh, well, there's plenty of time. Let's just see if it makes any difference to Miss Thorne. I doubt it, though. Her only stipulation was that she wants her mail brought up every day from the roadside box, and her trash can taken down on Thursdays when the garbage is collected. Any problem with that?"

"No, none," Elyn said.

"I believe Miss Thorne is badly crippled with arthritis and the house is set a long way from the road."

"That's fine, I can handle that," Elyn assured her.

"Okay, then. Come on, I'll take you out there so you can have a look."

The minute she saw it, Elyn knew. It was a perfect gem of a house. Exactly what she needed. The dining room could be turned into a studio; the smaller of the two bedrooms could be the nursery. The bathroom, aside from the claw-footed tub, had all new fixtures. The kitchen had golden birch cabinets, attractive hammered brass pulls, marbleized Formica counters, stainless steel sink, new stove.

More than that, the little house had a welcoming feel. If Miss Thorne agreed, maybe things were going to work out after all.

Chapter Four

The following morning Liz Miller gave Elyn the word that Miss Thorne had okayed the renting of the cottage at Meadowmead. Elyn wasted no time driving out to take possession of the little blue frame house. She felt happier than she had in a long time as she unloaded her car and carried all the boxes inside. Setting them down, she realized how little she had brought with her from San Francisco. She recalled the frantic way she had packed before leaving. Maybe she should have been more selective, not just filling up box after box and piling them into her car to take to the Goodwill store. She had wanted to get rid of anything that would remind her of Dex. Things he had given her, like the Swedish coffeemaker, the electric clock that gave the time, temperature and date. She had been ruthless, even with the more personal things like the Hermès bag and the designer scarves, the cashmere sweater and the amber beads. All went into boxes, helter-skelter, squashed down among her jogging pants, old paperback mysteries, lamps.

Now, as she emptied the boxes, she saw that she could have used some of the things she had so recklessly given away. Such basic household necessities as a can opener, frying pan and wastepaper baskets were missing and would have to be replaced.

Suddenly, Elyn had an anxiety attack. What had she done? What was she thinking? To come to a town where she knew no one, sign a year's lease on a house, cut herself off from everything familiar? Had she lost her mind?

Get busy, she commanded herself. The only way to avoid being overwhelmed was not to look back. She returned her attention to the boxes.

She had only been working at unpacking a short while when she heard a braking car outside. She brushed back a stray lock of hair and looked out the window. Maybe it was the telephone man here to hook up her phone. Instead she saw it was a blue pickup. A man got out. He was tall, broad-shouldered, long-legged in blue jeans. The collar of his denim shirt was open and the sleeves rolled up. He took off his billed cap and tucked it into his belt. His tawny hair was tousled and looked as if he could have used a haircut. He took the porch steps two at a time, gave a brief knock at the door left open from her last trip from the car and said, ''Hi. Getting settled?''

Elyn frowned. Who was this guy barging in like this? A neighbor? A salesman?

''Yes, I'm trying to,'' she said slowly, still trying to figure out who he might be. ''And you are?''

"I'm Doug Stevens."

Doug Stevens. For the third time in as many days the name had cropped up again. Now here he was in person. Larger than life, literally. Over six feet, he towered above her as he entered the house, looking around. His air of casual self-assurance was irritating.

"I did the restoration on this cottage, got it up to code so Miss Thorne could put it up for rent. It had been empty for quite a few years. So I just stopped by to see who'd moved in. I knew Miss Thorne was pretty particular about who she'd rent it to. You must have passed muster."

"Well, I must have. She gave me a year's lease," Elyn said a bit curtly.

Doug didn't seem to be put off by her coolness. He went right on talking. "Good! Miss Thorne hasn't been well these past few months. She's getting on in years and you just never know what might happen, when she might need someone. That's why I convinced her to let me fix up this place for a rental to someone reliable. I try to stop by every week or so when I'm in town to see if she's okay, take care of anything that might need doing."

Elyn felt her first impression of Doug changing. He must be a nice guy to have such concern for an elderly lady. "That's kind of you," she said, feeling suddenly sheepish about her earlier curtness.

"Not really. I'm real fond of Miss Thorne. She's a grand old lady. I guess you've found that out yourself."

"I haven't met her. The Realtor handled the deal."

Elyn had the distinct feeling that Doug Stevens had made a point of coming around to reassure himself. Make sure Miss Thorne's tenant passed *his* inspection. Anxious to end this unexpected interruption and get on with her unpacking, Elyn asked, "Is there something I can do for you?"

"No, but is there anything I can do for you? Everything okay here?"

"Fine. Everything's fine." She took a few steps over to the front door, hoping he would take the hint and leave.

"Good. I brought Miss Thorne down to take a look at everything. Liz Miller, too, before they listed the place. I like satisfied customers, lots of praise."

Elyn raised an eyebrow. Doug grinned.

He took a few steps to the door. "Well, glad everything's okay. Try to get up to the big house and make friends with Miss Thorne. I'm sure she gets lonely at times. When people live alone, it's good to know other people are living close by."

Annoyed at his assuming the right to give her instructions on neighborliness, Elyn snapped, "There aren't *people* living here, Mr. Stevens, just me."

His blue eyes twinkled. "That's what I mean. I hope *you* don't get lonely."

"That won't be a problem," Elyn retorted. Obviously he was on a fishing expedition.

Doug studied the ceiling, made another sweeping glance around. "Well, if you need anything to be done,

I'll leave one of my cards. It has my phone number on it. I know from working on the place, there are still things to be done...new vinyl floor in the kitchen...you'll need screens on the windows come summer. I'm not all that busy right now, so just let me know.''

The man was impossible. Why didn't he just go? Hardly concealing her impatience, Elyn took the card he held out to her, slipped it into her blouse pocket, then without looking at it said shortly, ''Thanks.''

Doug looked amused. He tugged the brim of his baseball cap as he put it on. ''Well, I'll be on my way.'' On the top step of the porch, he turned back, grinning. ''I'm going up to see Miss Thorne.''

Oh, sure, Elyn thought. Probably would race up the road and report what he had found out. Not much. She'd told him as little as she could. She hoped she hadn't made a mistake by moving to this small town. All she'd wanted was anonymity and, with luck, to find a way to make a living.

''I'll tell her we met, and that I approve of her choice of tenant.'' He started down the steps, then halted, turning back once again. ''By the way, I don't think I caught your name.''

Tempted to use the old cliché, ''I didn't drop it,'' Elyn quickly rejected the idea. Being funny might just encourage him, so she simply said, ''Elyn Ross.''

''Well, nice to have met you, Miss Ross. See you again.'' He ran down the rest of the steps and got into his truck. Elyn watched him back it around, then turn up the road that led to the big house.

Unreasonably annoyed, she shut the front door with a slam. She was sure she would be the hot topic of conversation. Still watching the truck, Elyn wondered if Doug Stevens had a key to this cottage. If he was such good friends with Miss Thorne, maybe he did. The thought made her uneasy. Maybe she would have the locks changed. Not because she found him threatening, but because she didn't like the idea of his having access to her house. Better first check with Miss Thorne. Elyn decided she should make a point of meeting her, so far elusive, landlady and ask her about it.

Elyn knew it was stupid to feel so irritated by someone she probably would never see again. No matter what went wrong in this little house while she was living here, she certainly didn't intend to call Doug Stevens to fix it.

Elyn might have stewed longer about her gentleman caller if Ronnie had not shown up. Her arms loaded with bags from the delicatessen and bakery, she came bounding in the door. "Hello, hello!"

She sat down her bundles, exclaiming, "Oh, Elyn, this is really marvelous!" She walked around, her four-inch heels clicking on the bare floors. "It just needs a little personalizing...you know, your own touches. It has lots of light and a wonderful view. For an artist, it should be great." She whirled around a couple of times. "As your first guest—"

"Actually you're not."

"What do you mean?"

"I had another one earlier. Uninvited and unwelcome."

"Who was that?"

"Doug Stevens."

"Really? He works fast. He came by the afternoon you and I met to ask about you. His exact words were something like 'Who was that knockout blonde with you today?'"

"Oh, please!" Elyn protested. "The last thing I need right now is to get involved with a man, Ronnie."

"Doug's a good guy. I'm glad you met. I mean, I know he checks on Miss Thorne regularly, and you never know when there might be some kind of an emergency."

"Let's change the subject."

"Okay. I just didn't want you to get the wrong impression of Doug. He's not some guy on the make."

Elyn made no comment.

"I brought you a housewarming gift. It's an old tradition—Jewish or Irish, I think. Not exactly sure which." She smiled and swung a basket up on the kitchen table. "A loaf of bread, a jar of honey and some salt. Symbols of my heartfelt wish. That you will never know want, that your life will have sweetness and be full of flavour." She gave Elyn a kiss on both cheeks. To her own amazement, Elyn burst into tears.

"Hey, what did I say? What did I do?" gasped Ronnie, looking distressed.

"Oh, it's not you. I'm sorry. I think I just..." Elyn

threw out both hands in a helpless gesture. "I think everything came down on me and I—"

"Can I do anything to help?"

"You already have, Ronnie. You've been super. I guess I suddenly freaked out. I haven't allowed myself to really think about what I'm facing. I mean, a *baby*. I never thought I'd go through this alone."

Stumbling a bit in places, Elyn told Ronnie a little about Dex, mostly about the last terrible scene. "I should have known better. I don't know what I was thinking. He accused me of trying to trap him into marriage. I denied it. But maybe, subconsciously, I did. You see, Ronnie, I was brought up in a Christian home. I always believed loving someone—I mean, intimately loving someone—meant marriage. Eventually. I loved Dex. At least, I thought I loved him." She drew a shaky sigh. "I loved the man I thought he was, but even that might have been my own need, I don't know." Elyn wiped her eyes with the backs of her hands. "So anyway, when I refused, told him I'd never have an abortion, well, that was the end."

Ronnie took both of Elyn's hands in her own and held them tight. "Elyn, I understand. Believe me, I do. I've been there. Listen, when I was a junior in high school, I thought I was madly in love. It seemed right, or at least not wrong enough to keep me from doing it. Anyway, my boyfriend kept saying, 'If you really loved me'— You know? Well, I got pregnant. And I was scared. When I told him, he accused me of being with someone else. He didn't want to have any part of the baby. I was afraid to tell my parents. It would have killed my mom and my dad. Oh, wow.'' Ronnie shuddered. "I don't know what my dad would have done. So…" She paused, her face anguished as if the memory still was painful. "I got the name of this person, and I went and I… It was awful. I could never tell anyone. My folks thought I was spending the weekend with my girlfriend. It was a nightmare. I was just lucky I didn't have any bad effects, no infection or anything. Nothing physical, that is. Emotionally, I've never gotten over it. It's been nine years, Elyn, and I still wake up in the middle of the night thinking it was just a bad dream. But it wasn't. That's why I think you're so brave.''

"But I'm not, Ronnie. I don't know how I'm going to make it. I feel so guilty. What if I can't make a living? It's like starting from square one. I let a lot of the promising possibilities I had right after art school go. After I met Dex, my career didn't seem that important. I guess I'm scared, unsure.''

"I understand how you feel, Elyn. Right now, it seems you're down for the count. But that's for the moment. I believe you've got a lot of talent you haven't even tapped into yet. There's an incredible amount of bounce in most of us.'' Ronnie squeezed Elyn's hands. "Take me, for example. This is the third time I've tried going into business for myself. Twice before I failed, had to go back to working for someone else for a while. But I always hated it because I knew I was creative and smart. If I could only pull it together, stick it out long enough, I could make it. Maybe the third time's the charm because The Crow's Nest is thriving.''

Elyn gave her a weak smile. ''The power of positive thinking, eh?''

''More than that. I don't know if you read the Bible or not, but there is a powerful psalm that says God wants to give us the desires of our heart and will if we trust Him. I'm doing what I love to do, Elyn, and making a living. Whatever you decide to do, I know you can, too.'' Ronnie gave Elyn a long, intense look. ''Well, now that we've bared our hearts to each other, how about putting on the kettle and making us some herbal tea?''

By the time Ronnie left that evening, it was nearly midnight. As they said good-night, Elyn realized their friendship had reached a deeper level. Although unburdening herself to Ronnie had given her some relief, Elyn knew there was a long, bumpy road ahead. She would need all the friends, all the faith, she had.

Chapter Five

She was wide-awake now, unable to settle for sleep. No matter how much she tried not to think about Dex and all that had happened, how could she not? He had been so much a part of her life and he was the reason she was here.

He was back from L.A. by now. What had he thought, she wondered, when he discovered she had left the city, closed her apartment, had her phone disconnected? Was he angry or relieved?

In spite of herself, Elyn's thoughts flashed back to the night they had met. Theirs had been a casual introduction at a party she had not even wanted to attend. She had gone with Tod Avery, one of the ad salesmen from the agency, whose own girlfriend, a stunning model, could not make it. Tod had prevailed on Elyn, insisting he could not show up alone at the gala, given by one of their new accounts at a posh hotel. Soon after they arrived, he had left her to work the room. Left to her own devices, Elyn had just been observing the party when someone she knew brought Dex over to be introduced. At the time no flares had gone up. She had not the slightest premonition that this meeting would change her life.

She recalled thinking only that Dexter Sherill was very good-looking. He had a lean, fine-boned face, sharply molded features, dark hair styled close to a well-shaped head. Of medium height and build, dressed in a superbly tailored gray suit, blue-striped shirt and paisley tie, he looked like a Montgomery Street investment broker, which he was.

Under his appraising glance, Elyn was glad she had taken more care than usual with her appearance that evening. She had worn a dress in a particularly becoming shade of blue. She had styled her hair in a French twist, which showed off the new silver-and-turquoise earrings a friend had brought her from New Mexico.

Later Dex told her it was her eyes he noticed first. "Bambi eyes," he called them. Large and velvety brown, an unusual combination with her fair skin and golden-wheat-colored hair.

After fifteen minutes or so of conversation, Dex had surprised Elyn by asking if she had come with anyone and if not, would she like to leave and go to dinner? She glanced at Tod who was happily occupied chatting with a pretty redhead. "Not really," she answered. As they passed Tod and Elyn signaled she was leaving with Dex, he lifted an eyebrow and smiled. Elyn knew he'd expect a report at the office the next day but didn't care.

Dinner with Dex that first time had been wonderful. He was charming, interesting and a perfect gentleman. He had taken her home and at the door invited her to go sailing the next Saturday.

That evening began his relentless pursuit. Her very naiveté spurred his imagination. He became obsessed to possess her.

At twenty-three, she had never had a serious relationship. She had been too poor, too busy putting herself through art school for much dating. Intent on her goal to support herself as an artist, she had not wanted to become involved in casual affairs like some of her fellow students. Elyn had held the values with which she had been brought up. She believed that intimacy led to commitment, commitment to marriage. Before Dex came into her life, marriage had been the farthest thing from Elyn's mind. Years in the future.

But she had been dazzled by Dex's sophistication and power, the excitement of the romance. It was the stuff of which romantic dreams were made—flowers, notes, phone calls, tickets to San Francisco shows of famous Broadway hits, dining out in elegant restaurants, the promises of the exotic trips they were going to take together…Mazatlan, Hawaii, Europe. Swept away by the glamour, Elyn had plunged into a passionate affair.

She'd thought she could have it all. A man who loved

her, marriage and an artistic career. But she had been wrong. Mostly, wrong about Dex.

The night she was sure she was pregnant, they were going to a gallery opening then on to dinner with some friends of his. She had dressed in a sleek black sheath Dex especially liked. It had a yoke and long sleeves of black lace. She wore black pumps with four-inch heels and the pearl pendant earrings he had given her.

The evening had been filled with rich food and sparkling drinks, and conversation punctuated with name dropping of prestigious people, places and resorts. During dinner Dex cast several curious glances at her as if puzzled or annoyed. Naturally she had been distracted, considering the secret she longed to share with him. Still she tried, as she always did, to please him, by entering into the conversation. It was afterward, when they were alone at his condo and she told him about the baby, that everything had fallen apart.

"Well, of course, you'll get rid of it."

"Get rid of it?"

"Of course." Dex frowned. "This wasn't in the game plan. I never planned on having children. Not with you, not with anyone."

She stared back at him, shocked.

His eyes darkened, hardened. "Of course, I'll pay for everything. Just make the necessary arrangements."

Elyn had felt a vise tighten around her throat, making it impossible to speak. She knew she could never do what he was demanding. Would never do it.

She could never forget the scene that followed. She saw a side of Dex she hadn't seen before. The suave veneer peeled away. She saw a hedonistic man, self-absorbed, selfish.

At last the tirade dragged out. Numbed, drained, disillusioned, Elyn told him she wanted to go home. He had called a taxi for her instead of driving her in his Mercedes to her apartment.

Through the long hours of that night Elyn alternately wept and paced. How could she not have seen this side of Dex before? How could she have been so blind? He had told her he loved her. If that was true, how could he have said the things he had? Demanded she do what he must know would be unthinkable to her?

The next morning Elyn faced reality. The scales had been ripped away from her eyes. The cruel things Dex had said were indelible. Things she couldn't forget or forgive. Their relationship had been a sham. Its foundation sand. The life she dreamed they would have together vanished into thin air. The fact that she had believed it possible was *her* mistake. There was no going back.

Alone in her bed, Elyn shuddered. The tears she had shed while confiding in Ronnie had released some of her emotion, but they had not lifted her burden of guilt. Even the fact that Ronnie suggested she find some comfort, some hope in the Scriptures, hadn't helped. It only made her feel guiltier.

It had been a long time since Elyn had been able to pray. During her affair with Dex, she had ignored her conscience, not wanting to be reminded of what she had been taught, that what she was doing was sinful. Sin was something you got punished for. Now surely she was "reaping what she had sown." How could God forgive her?

Finally, Elyn fell into an exhausted sleep and woke up unrested, unrefreshed. She drank two cups of decaffeinated coffee, then dug into the box of her art supplies and pulled out some of her sketchbooks. In her portfolio from art school she found some viable material. Greeting card companies were always looking for new talent for that hungry market. She chose a few she felt were good samples of her style and skill. She had the latest copy of *Artists' Market* and looked up the names of companies, studied their stated needs, and circled prospective matches with red ink. She would start sending her designs out.

She decided to follow Ronnie's advice to put an ad in the local paper. She spent the morning designing an eye-catching design and writing the copy to go with it.

In the meantime she already had one job, thanks to her new friend. Ronnie had ordered a new logo and business cards for The Crow's Nest.

Pleased with these first steps, Elyn knew she had to get on with her life, to build something from the shards of her broken dreams, to make a living for herself and her unborn child. The situation still seemed unreal, but Elyn knew only determination would make things right.

Chapter Six

Elyn was just settling at her drawing board and beginning to work when she heard the sound of tires on the gravel drive in front of the cottage. She went out to the front porch just as Doug Stevens was unloading some large cardboard boxes from the back of his truck. When he saw her, he smiled.

"Hi. These just came. Ordered them when I was doing the rest of the renovating, but they sent the wrong kind. Since I'm going to be gone for a few weeks, I thought I'd better put them in today, if that's okay. We're getting into some hot weather, so you'll need them installed."

"I don't know what you're talking about. Install what?"

"Ceiling fans. Miss Thorne never had air-conditioning put in, but these do pretty well, especially when both her house and this cottage are shaded by big oak trees." He started down the porch steps on his way back to the truck.

"Wait a minute! I don't—"

"No problem," Doug called back over his shoulder. "They're paid for. Not to worry. It'll take a little while and then you'll be all set."

"But, but—" Elyn's protest faded as Doug wrestled one of the boxes out of the truck bed. He came up on the porch, opened the screen door with one hand and went inside. Flustered, Elyn followed.

"I wish Miss Thorne had told me—"

Doug set down one box and walked right past her to go for the others. Frustrated, Elyn waited for him to come back into the house. "How long will it take?"

"Not long. Sorry, they were supposed to be in when you rented the place. You'll be glad once the temperature starts to heat up."

She went back to her drawing board, annoyed at the intrusion of her privacy. Why hadn't he at least called to see if it was convenient for him to come?

He stopped at her studio entrance, glanced over at the drawing board. "You just go on with whatever you were doing and I'll not bother you." He paused. "What were you doing?"

"Working."

"Working? Looks more like having fun." He glanced at her open paint box, colored pencils and markers.

"I'm an artist."

"Sure, I knew. I was just teasing. Ronnie told me you were very talented."

Elyn gave him a tight smile. "Ronnie tends to exaggerate."

"Well, anyhow, you go right ahead. I won't get in your way."

Elyn concentrated on the design she was sketching, trying to ignore him as he opened one of the boxes. But the man kept talking!

"You'll be glad when it's done, believe me. Valley summers can be plenty hot. Those poor guys who work in the city after that long commute appreciate coming home to a cool house for the weekend, right?"

"I wouldn't know. I'm not married." How unsubtle he was, trying to get information out of her.

He immediately changed tack. "Well, this is a great little house for someone single. Plenty of room, storage space, room for hobbies..." He halted after opening one of the boxes. "These fans are real efficient, keep things nice and cool. One of these will go in your guest room."

Elyn picked up her paintbrush, intent on ignoring him, then decided to satisfy his evident curiosity about her. "That's not a guest room. It's going to be a *nursery*."

Her brush poised, she watched his reaction.

He didn't miss a beat, just said, "Well, that too."

So now he knew she had no husband who would be down from the city for the weekend and that she was expecting a baby. Whether this surprised or shocked Doug Stevens, she couldn't tell. He went about his work, whistling under his breath. He was really too much. Elyn found it difficult to work as long as he was in the house. She found his presence disturbing.

For the next two hours there was a minimum of noise as Doug went about the business of installing the ceiling fans.

Elyn didn't get much done on her designs. If she had known beforehand about the installation, she could have arranged to be gone while it was being done. Now a good two hours of work had been wasted.

"All done," Doug's voice finally announced. "Just pull the cord when you want the air to circulate. If you have any problem, call me, okay?" His eyes teased as he added, "I believe you have my card."

Elyn blushed. She hadn't even looked at it.

"I won't be leaving until after the weekend, so call if you need me. Both my home phone and pager numbers are on the card." He gathered his tools and replaced them neatly in his toolbox. "Did I say I was going to Hawaii?"

Elyn hesitated. If she asked what was a natural follow-up question, it would just encourage him to tell her about his trip.

He told her anyway. "My parents retired to a small town near Kona, and I'm going over to do some remodeling for them. Mom has some ideas about her kitchen. You know women and their kitchens."

Elyn's mouth pursed. This man was really too much. "No, as a matter of fact, I don't. Never spent much time in kitchens. In fact, I can hardly boil water for instant coffee.''

He grinned. ''Well, you probably will when Junior arrives.''

Elyn did not return his smile.

''Well, so long. Enjoy your fans. Sorry to have disrupted your work.''

Doug left as abruptly as he had come. Watching the pickup go down the road, Elyn felt some belated embarrassment that she had been so ungracious. After all, he had put in the fans so she would be more comfortable. It was something he didn't have to do. She doubted if Miss Thorne had ordered them installed, or agreed to the expense.

Still, she could have at least thanked him properly to let him know she appreciated his kind gesture.

Chapter Seven

Within a short time some light was beginning to filter into the dark tunnel of Elyn's life. She'd established a daily schedule of working on her designs. And she meticulously carried out the terms of her lease, collecting the mail from the box next to hers at the end of the driveway and, on Thursday evenings, dragging Miss Thorne's garbage can down to the edge of the road.

Miss Thorne's mail was about as skimpy as her own. Utility bills and a few flyers of one sort or the other, together with the usual junk mail marked Occupant. When Elyn took the small batch up to the old house, there never seemed to be any sign of life.

Except for three cats, one a beautiful creature with a thick creamy coat, black markings and the telltale blue eyes of a Siamese mix, a calico tabby and a small nervous black cat who crouched, hissing at Elyn's approach, and which no amount of coaxing would allow Elyn to pet him. The three would line up along the porch steps while Elyn pushed the sheaf of envelopes through the brass letter drop, all the while speaking softly to the watchful trio.

One afternoon, as Elyn took Miss Thorne's mail from the box and walked up to the big house, she debated whether or not to ring the doorbell. She had been living in the little blue house for nearly a month. It seemed odd not to have met her landlady in person. She decided it was time to introduce herself, then take the opportunity to ask about the cottage keys.

But as she ascended the porch steps, the front door opened and a tall, gaunt woman, leaning on a cane, stood there. She wore a frayed cardigan, a blouse pinned at the neck with a beautiful cameo pin and a worn cotton skirt.

She brushed back a wisp of rusty-gray hair from her lined forehead and said in a husky voice. "I suppose you're my tenant."

Taken by surprise, Elyn nearly dropped the handful of mail. "How do you do, Miss Thorne. Yes, I'm Elyn Ross." She paused, then added, "I'm enjoying the cottage very much. Thank you for renting it to me."

"Hmph." Miss Thorne continued to regard her intently.

For a moment Elyn was uncertain whether to stay or simply go. It didn't seem a good time to bring up the matter of the keys. Neither did she feel she could just leave without some further communication. As she stood there, Elyn's artist's eye saw the remnants of beauty in Miss Thorne's sun-weathered face, now ravaged with deep wrinkles. But the woman's eyes were bright with interest and curiosity.

Finally Miss Thorne said, "Liz Miller tells me you're in the family way."

The quaint euphemism momentarily startled Elyn.

"Well, yes. I am expecting a baby in December. I didn't think you had any objections to renting to someone with a child?"

"Nonsense. No. Kids are fine. Should have had some myself." Miss Thorne sniffed. "Come in and have some tea and we'll get acquainted as long as we're neighbors." She stepped back and opened the door wider. "Elyn Ross. When I saw it on the lease Liz Miller brought me to sign, I thought it was a good, sensible, old-fashioned name." She gave a little laugh. "You know what mine is? No, you'd never guess. It's Lark. How's that for a fanciful name? And my sister's name was Robin. We had a fanciful mother. A sweetheart of a mother. And we had a wonderful childhood right here. Mama read a lot and was into fairies and a lot of things other adults thought right crazy. But we children loved it and loved her. I'm afraid I was rather a disappointment to her. But Robin made up for me. That's Robin." Miss Thorne gestured to a photograph of a beautiful young girl wearing long white gloves and a white ruffled gown with a bouffant skirt. "And that's Mama." She stopped to point to an oil portrait in the hall of a dainty, exquisite woman in an evening gown holding an ostrich fan.

Miss Thorne's parlor, along with the rest of the rambling house, was cluttered with museum-quality antiques. Silver-framed photographs covered every available space on the piano, tabletops and bookshelves. Tiffany lamps on molded metal bases gave the room its light, but the original vibrant colors of the masterpieces were filtered through inches of dust.

"I loved this place. Never wanted to leave, which goes to prove that old saying, 'Be careful what you wish for, you may get it!'" Miss Thorne laughed a crackly little laugh. "You see, I loved the freedom of life here. I wasn't the social butterfly my sister was for all my poor mother hoped. I wouldn't even go to Europe when I graduated from finishing school. My mother despaired of me. But she had my sister to launch. And Robin took to it all and did Mama proud. *She* was presented at court, with all the pomp of it and became one of the most popular American debutantes in London that year. She made a brilliant marriage to the son of a lord, although I don't think she was really happy.... Who knows?" Miss Thorne shrugged. "But then who is? Especially someone who lived out someone else's dream? I should be happy, come to think of it. I lived out my own dream. I think I've been reasonably happy. Content anyway. I guess that's all you can say when you reach my age."

The three cats had followed them out to the cavernous kitchen where Miss Thorne got delicate Havilland cups and saucers from a cabinet and put a kettle full of water to boil. "To answer your question about children, I guess you'd say these are my substitutes. Esme, Amber and Bette.''

That afternoon Elyn felt she had made a new friend. An unexpected one. As a matter of fact, she had befriended more than just the lady herself. The three cats had somehow intuited that Elyn was acceptable. After that day they took to coming down to the cottage for visits. Elyn found them fascinating subjects and often spent hours sketching them. Their bodies were so flexible, their movements so graceful. Her sketchbook was soon full of them in various poses. Sometimes, by some silent signal, all three got up and left, going back up to the big house. Not even putting out saucers of milk could entice them to stay if some instinct moved them to go.

Elyn learned a great deal about cats that summer, their total self-absorption, their aloof self-containment, their complete self-confidence.

She also learned a lot about herself. Somehow she'd been able to trust again, thanks to Miss Thorne, Ronnie—and even Doug—and to find inspiration when she'd thought none could be found.

Perhaps someday she could apply the lessons she was learning to help with raising her baby...and to help others.

Chapter Eight

For Elyn the long, sunny days of Valley summer produced a puzzling combination of physical lethargy and creative energy. She often took her portable easel and a canvas chair outside under the shade of the oak trees and tried to work. She was experimenting with various ideas, but had yet to come up with one she felt enthusiastic about. Most of the time she found herself simply sitting inert and drowsy from her progressing pregnancy, unable to put anything much on paper.

She wondered if Doug Stevens was back from Hawaii yet. For reasons she didn't want to explore, she had missed seeing his blue pickup going up and down the road to Miss Thorne's house. Even before he'd installed the ceiling fans, if he happened to pass her when she was returning from delivering her landlady's mail, he had always tooted his horn and waved. And the fans he'd so graciously installed were wonderful. Into full summer weather now, they provided a cool atmosphere in the house for her to work and sleep.

She stifled a yawn, debating whether to go indoors and take a nap when she saw the mail truck come and go. Deciding she needed exercise more than a nap, she collected Miss Thorne's mail and walked up the hill.

As usual, the mail consisted mostly of catalogs and flyers. As she walked up the hill, the afternoon sun was warm on her back. Her increased weight kept her pace leisurely. Elyn had always been slender and this new bulk had made her wonder if maybe she was having twins. Although there was no history of twins in her family, she didn't know about Dex. He had never talked about his family—or his background, for that matter. The more she thought about it, the more she realized how little she had really known about the man who was the father of the child she carried.

She dismissed the idea of twins. If that possibility had existed, certainly it would have shown up in the sonogram.

The three cats were snoozing on the porch in the sun, Amber curled up like a twist of butterscotch in a corner, Esme on the railing and Bette underneath one of the rockers. Elyn stopped to pet Esme, who languidly got up and stretched, turning her head so Elyn could rub her ears and the top of her head. Amber lifted her head, blinked, then resumed her nap. Elyn was about to slip the sheaf of mailings through the slot in the front door when it opened and Miss Thorne stuck her head out and asked, ''Want to come in for some iced tea?''

''Sounds good.''

"Sun tea," Miss Thorne said as she brought out the pitcher and added ice cubes and slices of lemon to float in the amber liquid. "I just drop in the tea bags, fill a jug with water and let it sit in the sun until it's brewed. It's not a bit bitter, just a nice strong flavor."

They sat in the rush-seated rockers, sipping their iced tea in companionable silence while watching the cats. Esme was perched on the porch railing, squinting watchfully, while pretending not to, at a few birds fluttering at the pedestal birdbath. Amber was curled up under one of the rockers in the shade. Black Bette was stretched out in the sun on the top step. Elyn wished she had her sketchbook.

Elyn finished her tea, replaced her empty glass on the tray on the wicker table, then got up reluctantly. "Thank you, Miss Thorne. That was delicious."

"Easy to make. You could do it, too. Before you go, Elyn, I want to give you something." Miss Thorne dug into her large handbag and pulled out a ring of keys, detached one and handed it to Elyn. "This is the key to the padlock on the gate up the hill behind my house. The path leads to a natural mineral springs pool. I want you to have this key, use the pool whenever you like. I can't make it up there anymore with my hip and legs in their condition. But it really is quite rejuvenating." She smiled. "You'd pay sixty dollars an hour to use something similar at one of those fancy spas."

"Why, thank you, Miss Thorne."

"You're more than welcome, and why don't you call

me Lark? 'Miss Thorne' seems too formal for neighbors.''

Elyn felt tears well in her eyes. This gesture of friendship touched her heart.

"I'd like that, Miss—I mean, Lark.''

As she walked back down the road to the cottage, Elyn marveled again at all the unexpected 'tender mercies' she'd received since coming to the Valley.

To Elyn's surprise, some weeks later Doug Stevens arrived unannounced. She saw the familiar blue truck pull to a stop in front of the cottage, and opened the door before he knocked. He seemed bigger, better-looking than she remembered. Tanned to a bronze, he looked wonderful, his eyes bluer, this teeth whiter, his hair sun-streaked.

"Hi, how're you doing?'' he greeted her. "Are the fans working okay?''

"Yes, just great. Thank you.''

"I thought they'd help.''

"By the way, I've met Miss Thorne,'' Elyn told him.

He nodded. "I know. She told me. She likes you. She doesn't take to many people or make friends easily. So that's a plus.''

Impulsively Elyn asked, "Would you like some iced tea? Miss Thorne's recipe.''

Doug hesitated. "Sure it won't…?'' He glanced at her drawing board.

"No. I'm through for the day.''

"Well, okay. Thanks. That sounds good."

As she got out ice, glasses, then poured the tea she had made earlier, she said, "Miss Thorne is certainly interesting. Entertaining. What stories she has to tell. The Valley must have been a much different place when she was young."

"Right. And she's one tough lady. I don't know exactly how much pressure she's had or what her financial situation is, but she has turned down all kinds of offers on her property. I mean six- and seven-figure amounts. The estate has a natural mineral spring and that's pure gold. City people are willing to pay any amount of money for their own spa. But she's stubborn. No offer's budged her yet."

While they drank their tea at her kitchen table, Doug was very open about himself in contrast to Elyn's reticence. He told her he had worked his way through college doing carpentry. Finding that he really liked building and being outdoors, he quit before getting his degree and studied on his own so he could pass the state exams and get a contractor's license. He'd come to the Valley five years ago and established his own business.

"I know you're an artist, but..." He glanced over at the drawing board, at the canvases stacked against the wall, the paints laid out on the small table beside it. "What exactly do you paint?"

"Flowers, ferns, little woodland creatures, children, cats."

"Ladies in flowered hats?" He kept looking at her, his eyes teasing.

"Occasionally."

"An impressionist style?"

"Not exactly. I'm a commercial artist, mainly. I'm hoping to sell designs to a greeting-card company."

"I see."

"I used to work for an advertising agency in—" Elyn stopped herself from being too specific. "But now I need to have a job I can do at home after I have the baby." She couldn't suppress a smile as she added, "That's why I don't spend much time in the *kitchen.*"

Doug winced and shook his head. "Don't hold that remark against me. It was—"

"I won't. Don't worry."

They both laughed.

Doug took a long swallow of his tea. "Boy, that tasted wonderful. Thanks." He got to his feet. "Well, I better be on my way."

Elyn walked to the door with him and stood on the porch as he bounded down the steps, then hopped into his truck. She watched him drive down the road, glad she had made the friendly gesture. Doug Stevens, as Ronnie had once told her, was one of the good guys.

Chapter Nine

Indian summer lingered in the Valley late into September. On her way home from a doctor's appointment in the nearby town of St. Helena, Elyn mulled over what her obstetrician had told her. Dr. Alers assured her that everything about her pregnancy was proceeding well. "But first babies sometimes come late," she'd told Elyn with a smile.

Elyn realized she better start doing some practical things to get ready for the baby. She also decided to begin fixing the other bedroom up as a nursery. Her imagination was suddenly flooded with ideas for buying unfinished furniture—a bureau and toy box, maybe—to paint with her own fanciful designs. The more she thought about it, the more excited she got, and the more real the baby became.

It was a perfect fall day. During the drive to Calistoga, she passed roadside stalls piled high with autumn produce—turban squashes, yellow and green zucchini and pumpkins of all sizes and shapes, plus bushel baskets of apples. She needed to pay more attention to her diet, so she stopped and bought some luscious tomatoes, yellow squash and apples.

A little farther along the road she saw a sign that read We Buy Junk and Sell Antiques. Amused, Elyn pulled over and wandered in among an eclectic assortment of old furniture and collectibles.

In one corner she spotted a rocker. It had several coats of peeling paint and a collapsed seat, but the back and arms were a lovely shape and it was just the right size. The price was an unbelievable eight dollars.

The store's owner carried it out to the car for her, then shook his head when he saw her small compact. "I don't know, lady," he said doubtfully.

Just then a familiar blue pickup swerved to a stop behind her car. To Elyn's astonishment Doug got out. He explained he was returning from the building site he was working on in St. Helena when he saw Elyn. Hearing the problem of getting the chair into Elyn's small trunk, he suggested putting the rocker in the back of his truck to deliver to the cottage for her.

Gratefully Elyn accepted the offer. As she followed him the rest of the way home, she wondered if there was some way she could thank him for coming along at just the right time.

When they got to the cottage, Doug jumped out of his truck before she had time to get out of her car. He came over to her and leaning into the window said, "Look, Elyn, there are umpteen coats of paint on that chair."

"I know. I plan to remove them."

"Those paint removers are real toxic. I don't think it's a good idea for you to be around that kind of stuff when you're expecting. Could do some damage to you or the baby. So let me take it and get it down to the wood—I think it's a pretty good grade of oak. We can easily replace the seat, tighten the legs—it'll be a neat chair."

"That's awfully kind of you, Doug."

"No problem. I've got all the equipment, a place to work. Okay?"

"Why, yes, thank you very much." Elyn was touched by his thoughtfulness.

Doug glanced into the back of her car, loaded with the day's other purchases.

"Let me give you a hand with those," he said. Without waiting for a response, he opened the door and started pulling out packages. Elyn walked ahead of him, up the porch steps and unlocked the front door.

"Won't you come in? I can fix you a cup of coffee."

"Thanks, but I'll take a rain check. How about when I bring back the chair?"

"Of course. And thanks, Doug."

"Glad to be of help."

A few days later Doug showed up with the chair.

"It looks wonderful," Elyn exclaimed. "Brand-new."

"Well, not exactly. That's not what you wanted, is it?

I figured you liked the idea of an old-fashioned rocker.'' Doug ran his hand along the smooth surface of the fan back and the curved arms. ''Nice wood.''

''Would you like that cup of coffee?'' she asked. ''It's decaf.''

His smile broadened. ''Sounds great.''

He followed Elyn into the kitchen.

''Instant, okay?''

''Fine. No cream.'' A minute later she placed two mugs on the table and sat down opposite him. Looking across at her, Doug thought Elyn looked different from that first time he'd met her. Her features were softer somehow, her skin still slightly tanned from summer. Her hair was longer now, worn back from her oval face, making her incredible eyes huge. Her wrists, exposed under the rolled-up cuffs of her plaid flannel shirt, looked fragile.

He glanced at her ringless hands cupping the coffee mug. What kind of a man had abandoned her? Could she still be hung up on him? Doug had tried to find out more about her from Ronnie, but Ronnie staunchly refused to reveal anything but the most rudimentary information about her friend. ''When you know Elyn better, you can ask her yourself,'' she'd said.

But how did a guy like him get to know someone like Elyn Ross, who was beautiful, sensitive and an artist? She didn't make it easy. She kept herself aloof...an ice princess. Why? Was she afraid to trust anyone... especially a man?

Doug was curious, and definitely interested. But this wasn't the right time. And who knew, after the baby she might just up and leave the Valley as mysteriously as she had come.

He warned himself to be careful, to tread lightly. He didn't want to make a false move. Say the wrong thing. Act too eager, move too quickly.

"Well, I've got to be on my way," he said, then shoved back his chair and stood up.

"Thanks again for the chair, Doug."

"I liked doing it."

They said goodbye and Doug left. Elyn gave the chair a push and it rocked smoothly. Tentatively she sat down in it, trying to imagine how it would feel to sit here rocking with a baby in her arms. After a while she put the rocker into the room that would soon welcome its little occupant, then went out and closed the door.

As she settled back down to her drawing board, she realized she had jumped to conclusions about Doug Stevens. He'd certainly gone out of his way to be helpful and friendly. Maybe he didn't have the suaveness of someone like Dex, but he had a genuine generosity. Both Lark and Ronnie had told her so. And now she'd come to know that herself.

Chapter Ten

The beautiful fall weather continued and although her pregnancy made Elyn's daily walks up to Lark's take longer, it was a time for the two of them to visit. This day, Lark was sitting on the porch in the sunshine when Elyn arrived.

"Afternoon. Beautiful day, isn't it? I think this is the prettiest time of the year in the Valley except for spring. But I say that about every season. I enjoy them all." Then she said, "Come sit down. I want to ask you a favor. I think I told you I didn't renew my driver's license, didn't I? *I* wanted to make the decision not to renew rather than allow the DMV to decide for me," she added with raised eyebrows. "Anyway, I wondered how you'd feel about driving me to church next Sunday? It's St. Francis Day, and they're having a special blessing of the animals. You know he was a great lover of all creation, the sun, the moon, the stars, as well as the birds and the bees. All of God's creatures, small domestic an-

imals, donkeys and cows, the whole kit and kaboodle.''
She gave another little laugh. "You probably know some
of the beautiful poems he wrote? No? Well, he was a
poet as well as a saint." Miss Thorne leaned on her cane.
"I'd like to take my girls in to be blessed, but I don't
think I can manage all three by myself, so I got to thinking you might help me. I think you'd enjoy the service.
It's quite unique. And the blessing is for all God's creatures—your baby, too."

Touched, Elyn replied, "Sure, I'd be happy to do
that."

"Well, good. I'll have Esme on her leash. She's been
before and knows how to behave. Amber and Bette will
have to go in their carriers. You can manage one of them,
don't you think?"

"Of course."

"The service is at ten, so it would be best if you came
up here a little after nine. We might have a bit of trouble
coaxing Bette into the carrier. She's not used to being
hauled around even if it's for a good reason."

Walking down the hill a short time later, Elyn was
pleased that Miss Thorne had asked her to attend something that evidently meant a great deal to her. The very
fact that the independent old lady had asked her help was
certainly a token of their growing friendship.

On Sunday morning, Elyn woke up early. In recent
months finding a comfortable way to sleep had become
somewhat of a problem. She often awakened and found
it easier to get up and move around.

On this particular day she had to decide what to wear to church. None of her dresses fit anymore, and the clothes she favored now, mostly maternity pants and oversize shirts, were not suitable for church. She knew the Episcopal church required more traditional attire than some of the other ones who held more casual services.

She finally decided on a loose jumper she had bought on impulse last summer on sale. Over a long-sleeved pastel T-shirt, it would do. She also had a straw hat bought on a whim at a street fair which she had never worn. She grabbed some late blooming marguerites from outside and tucked a tiny bunch into the hat's ribbon band, completing her outfit.

Miss Thorne, in a flowered dress and a wide-brimmed hat, was ready and waiting for her when she arrived at the big house.

With far less trouble than Elyn would have anticipated, they got Amber and Bette into their carriers and placed on the back seat. Miss Thorne, carrying Esme, got into the passenger seat of Elyn's car and they started off.

In town there were already a number of cars parked along both sides of the street in the vicinity of St. Luke's. After circling the block twice, Elyn decided the best thing to do was to let Miss Thorne and Esme out in front of the church, then she would find a parking place and follow with the two other cats in their carriers.

A few streets away she found a spot and quickly swerved into it. She wrestled the two carriers out of the back seat and set them on the grass for a minute while she adjusted her hat. Both cats were loudly complaining about their situation. Elyn hoped they would quiet down once they got to the church.

It was a futile wish because the closer she got to St. Luke's, the louder the plaintive meows became. She need not have been worried, however. Many of the other animals brought by their owners for this special blessing did not seem too happy about it, either. There were a wide variety of owners and pets gathered outside the church forming a line to enter.

There were people holding birdcages, cuddling puppies or snuggling cats. Among the crowd were children with rabbits and gerbils. All breeds of dog were represented from toy poodles to Great Danes. Elyn had never seen such an assortment and never heard of such a service. She saw Miss Thorne with Esme, nestled in the crook of her arm. The Siamese, a veteran of this ritual, seemed to be looking rather condescendingly at the motley array around her. Miss Thorne waved Elyn forward and she made her way through the crowd to join her.

''Come, Elyn, we'll go in. A friend is saving a place for us in her pew up front.''

At the door, a smiling, bald-headed man handed out folders on which was printed ''Welcome to St. Francis Day Service.''

When they reached their seats, Elyn put the two carriers on either side of her. Miss Thorne had stuck some small cat nibbles through the vents and Amber and Bette were momentarily appeased.

Around them, the noise level rose as the voices of the congregation mixed with animal sounds of all kinds. Elyn chanced a look behind her and saw that people with larger animals, mostly those with dogs on leashes, were lined up in the back.

Filled with curiosity about how all this was going to take place, Elyn straightened as the deep chords of the organ sounded. A young cleric in a starched white surplice came to the middle of the altar and smilingly extended both hands.

"Let us sing the hymn printed in the pamphlet you were given at the door." There was a great rustling and shuffling as people got to their feet. Elyn had never heard the hymn before, but to most of the congregation it seemed familiar.

When the last note faded away, the minister announced, "Now, all those with animals to be blessed, please come forward. Let the children come first, then they may be dismissed and we will have a short prayer service."

Elyn felt her throat tighten, watching the parade of children move toward the steps of the altar, clutching their pets or leading them. The minister leaned forward, placing his hands on the head of the animal, asking each child in a quiet voice the name of the pet.

It was simple, but very moving. The children filed out in the side aisles and finally the church became quiet. Then the minister spoke again.

"And now I will give a general blessing to those who

have pets with them. You can remain seated and accept it for your pet by name. Lord, we ask your blessing on these your creatures that they will know good health, that they will be treated with gentle hands and kind words, bring comfort and happiness to their owners.''

A few minutes of silence followed, then was broken by the minister's voice again.

''All of you who have come today have shown a strong degree of faith in honoring the loving legacy of Francis who was known, even in his own day, to manifest love for all God's creatures. One of my favorite Scriptures is Matthew 6:26. 'Consider the birds of the air, they neither sow nor reap nor gather into barns, yet your Heavenly Father feeds them. Are you not of more value than they?' God truly cares for us just as much or more than His other creatures. We are not to worry but to trust. In another beautiful passage, we are told 'not a sparrow falls,' but the Father knows. In turn we must show love to the creatures he has put into our care. That is why today is so special. It reminds us of God's loving care and provision for each of us. So now I say, go in peace, and God love and bless you all.''

Unexpectedly a slow warmth spread through Elyn, leaving her almost limp with peace. She had come today merely to accommodate Miss Thorne. She knew little about St. Francis, nothing about his blessing. Yet the minister's words seemed to be spoken directly to her. She had been constantly worried about how she was going to manage once her small amount of money dwindled. How she would be able to support herself and her baby. Concerned that her artwork would not bring in enough. She had been touched by his reading of the verse from Matthew. Are you not of more value than they? Surely, the Lord cared for her as much as the birds of the air? If she could only believe that. Believe He had forgiven her. If she could only learn to trust Him.

Miss Thorne leaned toward her and whispered, "Well, what did you think?"

"I thought it was beautiful."

"I'm glad." Miss Thorne caressed Esme's head. "And the girls were pretty well behaved, don't you think?"

"Yes, they were at that." Elyn laughed.

Outside the church, several ladies clustered around Miss Thorne, expressing their delight to see her, asking if she'd been unwell, why she hadn't been attending services.

"Not for lack of wanting to," she answered with her usual asperity. "Lack of transportation. Didn't renew my driver's license. So I asked my new neighbor, Elyn, if she'd like to come and she said she'd drive me. Have you met her? Elyn Ross."

"No, I don't believe I have." One of the women to whom Miss Thorne had been speaking glanced at Elyn, her eyes moving over her. "How do you do?" Her pointed gaze stopped at Elyn's left hand, her ringless third finger, then moved to her rounded figure. "How do you do?" she repeated coolly. Then she turned back to

Miss Thorne and continued talking. "Weren't the flowers lovely this morning? Of course, you used to do them beautifully, Lark, when you were active in the Altar Guild. I remember the big, beautiful bouquets of lilacs and hydrangeas you brought from Meadowmead. These, of course, were florist arrangements. For the Thomason girl's wedding yesterday. A lovely one, very traditional. The bride was simply a picture—orange blossoms, lace veil, the train on her dress a yard long. It's so gratifying to see how *some* young people are going back to the cherished values, isn't it?"

Her glance again took in Elyn, then she looked away. Another lady came to join the chatter, then eventually everybody said goodbye and dispersed to their own cars.

After arranging the cats comfortably, Miss Thorne got into the passenger seat beside Elyn. "I hope you weren't offended by Lu McClure. She rattles on a great deal and doesn't pay too much attention to what she's saying."

Elyn smiled. "The one regaling the virtues of renewed values? No, not at all. I'm sure they noticed I'm pregnant and there's no husband in evidence. My grandmother feels the same way." Elyn sighed. "I just hope you weren't embarrassed. Actually, I didn't think about that when you asked me to come with you."

Miss Thorne reached over and patted Elyn's hand. "Neither did I and I wasn't. Not a bit. You're my friend, Elyn. That's all that matters."

As Elyn backed out of the parking space, she thought how Miss Thorne had never asked her any questions about her situation. Never probed for details. She had accepted her and they had become friends, each respecting the other's privacy. It was really quite remarkable.

It wasn't until they were on the country road heading out to Meadowmead that either of them spoke. Elyn broke the silence.

"You know, it's really ironic. I always dreamed of having a church wedding. From the time I was a little girl, I loved the idea. The Christmas I was five, I asked for a bride doll and when I got to the Barbie stage, my girlfriend and I always played weddings. She had a Ken doll so that was fine. My Barbie got to be the bride." She smiled, reminiscing. "I just always thought that when I grew up, I'd have a beautiful wedding and live happily ever after in a dream house." She gave a rueful laugh. "I certainly didn't think I'd end up an unwed mother!"

"Life has a way of changing things for us" was Miss Thorne's only comment. Elyn was grateful. That was what she liked about Miss Thorne. She never offered any advice nor made banal remarks.

At the big house, Elyn helped her neighbor with the cats who meowed with glee when they were set free from their carriers.

"Well, I'm off for a nap," Miss Thorne declared. "I'm exhausted. Thank you for driving me to church."

"You're more than welcome. I enjoyed it."

Later, when she was back in her cottage, Elyn looked at the pamphlet from the day's service again. On the back was a poem. Its title was the same hymn they'd sung, "All things Bright and Beautiful." The author's name was Blanche Handler.

Elyn cut out the poem and put it on her refrigerator where she could see it every day—in particular for those inevitable times when worry or unease about her future assailed her.

Chapter Eleven

Elyn tried hard to hold on to the peace she had felt after the service at St. Luke's. But in spite of her efforts, in spite of the affirming message on her refrigerator door, anxiety seemed to pounce whenever she did not consciously try to be positive. The constant strain of trying to get something going with her artwork caused a feeling of stress. And she was concerned how her stress might affect the baby.

She desperately wanted to be a good mother. No matter what the circumstances of its conception and birth, she wanted her baby to feel loved and welcomed.

She had sent some of her designs to two greeting card companies weeks ago. Every day she checked the mailbox for some reply. Maybe her designs weren't good enough, not professional enough. Maybe they looked amateurish and would be rejected. Those companies probably got hundreds of submissions. Why did she think *hers* would be accepted?

Elyn felt depressed and restless. She tried to work at her drawing board, but ended up making mostly meaningless squiggles. This wouldn't do. She should be making this time productive. After the baby, what then? Unless something happened soon—

Suddenly everything crashed in upon her. All her mistakes. How foolish she had been. Why hadn't she seen what a disaster her relationship with Dex was, how wrong it was, that it was leading nowhere? It was her own fault. She was as responsible as Dex for what had happened.

From far back in her memory of Sunday school, the phrase *age of accountability* came to mind. She *was* accountable. There was no one to blame but herself.

Elyn thought she had cried all her tears. However, she began to cry. Great choking sobs. For all she had forsaken, for all she had abandoned, for all that she had recklessly thrown away.

Finally she wiped her eyes, splashed her face with cool water and told herself this must stop. Tears were wasteful. She should be thinking positively, planning, pursuing work.

She raised her head and saw the key to the mineral pool Miss Thorne had given her. She had hung it on the nail by the back door.

The day was summer warm. Why not go up to the mineral pool? If ever she needed quiet and relaxation, it was today.

She took the key and walked up the hillside until she

came upon a sagging wire fence. When she inserted the key into the rusty padlock, it stuck. It took some twisting for it to give. The gate opened with a grating squeak. A winding path, almost overgrown with tangled blackberry vines and long grass, led farther up.

As she climbed to the crest of the hill, Elyn wondered how long it had been since anyone had been up here. Ahead of her she saw a curved bridge, with trellises on either side and wisteria forming a ceiling overhead. She paused to look at the bridge, for it reminded her of pictures she had seen of one like it in Monet's garden.

After crossing the bridge, she found herself in a sheltered grotto of mountain stone, the pool in the center. Down one side, a waterfall poured into the pool which rippled with tiny bubbles.

She sat on the edge of the pool and gingerly eased herself into the water. It was a delightful surprise. The water was warm. She lowered herself until her shoulders were covered. Letting herself go, she drifted to the other side. There, she pressed her back against the smooth stone, tilted her head and looked up at the sky, which was a seamless blue through the foliage of the aspen trees surrounding the pool. With a sigh, she released all the troubling thoughts that had plagued her and let them whirl away with the rippling water. Elyn closed her eyes. The only sound was the gentle splash of the waterfall and an occasional birdsong high above in the trees.

She hummed the melody of an old hymn that came

into her mind. Effortlessly her arms and legs trailed in the water.

As the buoyancy of the water took away the weight of her body, so did her heart feel a lightness of spirit. Surely God had seen her remorse, surely He looked with mercy and compassion on her past mistakes. He knew her heart, that she had made the only choice she could, even though it meant bringing a child into the world by herself. The worst thing she had done was to deliberately do something she knew would take her out of grace. As if God didn't know.

Grandma had read the Bible out loud every morning at breakfast before Grandpa had gone to work and Elyn to school. The words had fallen on Elyn's ears even when she was thinking of something else, like the new sweater she wanted or the guy on the football team she hoped would ask her out.

The Word of God is a two-edged sword. Those words rang a bell in Elyn's heart. How strange that after all these years, how far away she had drifted, Scripture once again reminded. "My Word...shall not return to me void, but it shall accomplish what I please, And it shall prosper in the thing for which I sent it."

Elyn's heart quickened. Isaiah 55:11. She was remembering this particular Scripture for a purpose. God's purpose. Her lips began to move and she prayed the sinner's prayer she had heard dozens of times at the weekly altar calls in the church where she and her grandparents had worshiped when she lived with them.

Tears rolled down her face, fell into the bubbling water swirling around her. Gradually Elyn felt a peace she thought she had lost forever.

When she got out of the pool, toweled off and started down the hill to the cottage, Elyn knew something had happened. Something wonderful and special. She didn't understand it, but somehow she knew she could go on.

Chapter Twelve

After that day at the pool, Elyn felt a new kind of resolve. She had also gained a little encouragement from the acceptance of two of her card designs by a small company. There had been an accompanying letter saying they would be interested in seeing more of her work. She renewed her efforts to create designs, convinced that if she hoped to have a steady income from her work, she would have to establish herself by submitting new designs regularly. She was determined to succeed. The alternative had too many negatives to consider. Failure was not an option. Not if she wanted to achieve her goal to work at home, and make a living for herself and her child.

One evening a few days later, Ronnie called, suggesting she pick up a pizza and bring it out to spend the evening. Elyn was delighted. She had worked hard all day at the drawing board and was not too happy with the results. Ronnie was always so cheerful and full of interesting things to tell her, she knew it would be a real lift.

When Ronnie arrived, Elyn put the pizza in the stove to keep warm while she boiled water for tea. From her vantage point in the kitchen Elyn saw Ronnie wander into the room she used as her studio, checking some of the canvases stacked facing the wall that Elyn had brought with her from San Francisco. One by one, Ronnie turned them over, studying them. It made Elyn a little nervous. Some of them were experimental things she had done in art school. Others were pieces she had done during the spurts of creativity since she was pregnant. Elyn had always been shy about showing her paintings to anyone. Student exhibits at art school had always been agonizing for her.

Feeling uncomfortable at the scrutiny of her work, she called to Ronnie, "Our tea's almost ready."

Ronnie remained standing a minute longer, gazing at a particular painting before joining Elyn in the kitchen. After pouring each of them a mug of the fragrant herbal tea and adding a spoonful of honey to her own, Ronnie asked, "What do you intend to do with all those paintings?"

Elyn shrugged. "Goodness knows. Paint over them, most likely."

Ronnie's eyes widened. "I hope you're kidding. You have at least a half dozen really good paintings there that would sell." Ronnie took a sip of her tea, added more honey, stirred it.

"Oh, Ronnie, I'm not that good. Not yet, anyway.

With all the galleries exhibiting professional artists here, why would anyone buy mine?''

Her expression stern, Ronnie looked at Elyn. ''I know what people are looking for when they browse in my shop, Elyn. Pretty decorative pictures for the living room or bedroom or children's rooms. Something catches their eye and bingo—they buy it.''

She held up her hand to ward off Elyn's skeptical head shake.

''I was looking at the ones of the funky Victorian houses. They're so bright and colorful and full of life. But that's San Francisco, right? The homey ones of porches with white wicker furniture and pots of geraniums, lobelia and Shasta daisies—those are the kind of paintings people love. The kind you paint.''

''Thank you, Ronnie. That's kind of you to say but—''

''I'd like them for my shop, Elyn. Look, I'll have them framed and that can be my gallery percentage. If I'm wrong, no harm done, all right?'' Her eyes twinkled. ''But I have a hunch I'm right.''

''I'm not sure I should let you go to that expense. What if they don't sell?''

''If they don't sell, they'll look great in the shop. That's what customers enjoy about The Crow's Nest, finding unexpected things. I've never had paintings in it before.''

''Well, if you really want to try.''

''I do. Trust me. Now, how about the greeting card designs?''

"Oh, Ronnie, I'm so excited. I just sold two of my designs. And my editor said she would be willing to look at any others I had, though she's seen too many chipmunks, bunnies and birds. But I haven't been able to come up with any new ideas. I've done a number of sketches, but I'm not exactly certain of what to do with them."

"You mean Miss Thorne's cats? I noticed the ones on your drawing board and the sketches on the wall above it. They're great. There is something…I don't know… sort of mysterious about them. Not warm and fuzzy like some of the other card designs you've shown me."

"I know what you mean. I think so, too. They wouldn't be right for the kind of greeting cards she's interested in buying."

"Remember when studio cards first came out?" Ronnie said. "Humorous plays on words? A twist of some kind on the usual greeting?"

"Yes, but they only appealed to a small number of card buyers. Of prime importance to acquisition editors is what they call 'sendability.' A card with the widest, largest target buyer. Only a few offbeat type cards ever really go."

They were both silent for a moment, thinking. Then Ronnie said, "Mmm, that wonderful smell. Our pizza must be ready."

Both women returned to the kitchen where Elyn rescued the pizza from the oven, then placed the salad she had made beforehand on the table. They sat down to eat and to continue their discussion.

Holding a piece of pizza a few inches from her mouth, Ronnie mused, "Your sketches are too good to waste, Elyn. There must be some type of card they would be just perfect for."

Elyn nodded. "I spend a lot of time watching Esme especially, and she's so cool, so...so..." Elyn's voice drifted off as she searched for the right descriptive word.

They were both quiet for a long while, brows knitted, eyes squinted as they gave the matter more thought.

"Perhaps if we did a kind of cliché reversal," Ronnie began, visibly excited. "We could put the familiar part with the cat on the front, then you'd open the card and get a surprise one-liner. For instance..." Ronnie closed her eyes as if in a trance waiting for inspiration. "Something like 'Absence makes the heart grow fonder' on the front, then inside a snippy little cat saying something like 'Don't count on it!'"

They both dissolved into laughter.

"Yes! That's marvelous!" Elyn exclaimed.

They began throwing out one ridiculous idea after another.

"Go get some paper and a couple of pencils so we can write these down before we forget them." Ronnie giggled. "Of course, some of these are too ridiculous or awful. But if we could come up with even a half dozen good ones to put with your sketches, you could send them out. If not to the company who took your other ones, then to some other company.''

"Oh, Ronnie, do you really think people would go for them, or is it just us nuts?''

"The world is full of nuts.'' Ronnie laughed.

They spent the next hour coming up with crazy punch lines, one more outrageous than the next.

"Do you really think people will buy these?'' Elyn asked again, wiping her eyes after coming up with a hilarious response to one of Ronnie's quips.

"People will love them!'' Ronnie assured her. "I can already think of a dozen people I'd send one of these to, can't you? All the people who snubbed you, or didn't call back, or that nerd in junior high who didn't show up to take you to the prom!''

"I don't think they should be mean, just funny.''

"No, of course not. We'll self-censor. But it's just therapeutic to make up a list of people to send one to, isn't it? What shall we call them? They've got to have some kind of name. Something that clicks in a purchaser's mind. What do they ask for when they walk into a shop looking for this certain kind of greeting card?''

"Yes. A line should have its own identity.'' Elyn closed her eyes, knitted her brow. "I've always thought cats were haughty, with a kind of royal aloofness—sort of sophisticated, you know?''

Suddenly, Elyn bounced in her chair. "I know! What about 'Sophisticats'?''

"Perfect! That's it. Sophisticats." Ronnie jumped up, spun around, and they both laughed hysterically.

When Ronnie left later that evening, she took five of Elyn's paintings along, promising to show them to her when they had been framed. At the door she shook a playful finger at Elyn. "We're going to make you a millionaire with Sophisticats. Now get to work!"

"Don't worry, I will. This is too good an idea to sit on."

Too excited about the new line of greeting cards, instead of going to bed Elyn spent an hour or so at her drawing board, looking through her sketches, selecting ones she could submit. She decided to stylize the figures of the cats, choosing Esme as a model. Because of her Siamese markings, she was the epitome of cat aristocracy. Elyn elongated Esme's limbs, enhanced her slanted blue eyes, and gave her small triangular face a more aloof expression. Yes, that was it! She *had* "got it." Sleepy but satisfied, she turned off the light over the drawing table and went to her room where she fell into bed.

Convinced that Sophisticats was an inspired idea, Elyn smiled in the dark and murmured a prayer of thanks. In spite of her weak faith, the Lord, as was promised in Scriptures, had provided her with an idea when she needed it most. His goodness was above all she could think or ask.

Chapter Thirteen

Beautiful bright October had long since gone. November ushered in chilly, damp weather and overcast skies. December followed with more of the same. Elyn hardly noticed, she was so busy working on her new designs.

With the birth of Sophisticats she now had a point and purpose to her day. A reason to get up in the morning and work at her drawing board.

Increasingly some of her other more traditional card designs had sold and the card company who bought them wanted more. All of this gave her confidence that things were going to work out, that by the time she had the baby she would have a steady income from her designs.

On a gray, drizzling morning the third week in December, Elyn had just settled at her drawing board when a knock sounded at the door. Maybe it was the UPS bringing some baby things she had recently ordered from a catalog. Basic layette items. With a sigh she got up awkwardly. Her increased bulk made quick movement difficult. But when she opened the door, it was not a delivery man. It was Doug Stevens.

"Hi," he greeted her. "I just finished a job and when we were doing the cleanup, there was a lot of leftover wood...good kindling and some nice firewood. Thought you could use it. I know that little stove you have uses plenty of wood and this house isn't insulated—although it should be. That's one of the jobs I could do next spring. Anyway, I thought I'd just stack the wood here on the side porch so it's easy to get to, if that's okay?"

Not waiting for her to answer, he began unloading his pickup which was backed up to the porch. Speechless at his unexpected arrival, Elyn remained standing in the doorway, watching him make quick work of the job.

When he finished neatly placing the last log, he wiped his forehead with the back of his forearm and grinned at her. "There you go, all set."

"That was awfully nice of you."

"No problem. Don't like to see things go to waste."

"Well, come on in anyhow. Have a cup of decaf. Instant, of course." They both laughed.

"You made me an offer I can't refuse." Doug grinned and ventured into the kitchen with her.

As he removed his jacket and settled himself in a chair, he asked, "How's the greeting card business going?"

"Good, I hope. I've made a few sales and I'm working on a new idea."

She poured him a mug of coffee and got milk out of

the refrigerator. "No cream, I'm afraid. Skim?" She held the carton up questioningly.

"That's okay." He held out the mug for her to top off.

Doug took a sip of coffee. "Got any plans for Christmas?"

"A few." Elyn lowered her eyes. Her long lashes made dark crescents on her cheeks.

He wondered what kind of plans. There had been no wreath on the front door, and when he followed her into the kitchen he'd noticed a spindly table-size tree as yet untrimmed. Didn't look like any signs of holiday decoration.

Doug could have kicked himself for asking the question. In all the months since she had lived at the cottage, Elyn never seemed to have much company. Had she made any other friends here but himself, Ronnie and Miss Thorne? He couldn't think of anything else to say. Of course, when she had the baby, she would be busy.

He felt uneasy. He'd better get going before he put his foot in his mouth again.

He glanced at Elyn and suddenly his heart turned over. She looked so small, so vulnerable somehow. He wished he could do something to make things better for her.

"And you?" she asked.

"Me?" Her question startled him. "Oh, I'm going to spend the holidays with my parents. It's kind of a double celebration. Their thirty-sixth wedding anniversary. Big party. My brother and his family will be coming, too."

"When are you leaving?"

"Matter of fact, day after tomorrow. Looking forward to some sunny weather for a change."

"Lucky you."

"Have you ever been to the islands?" he asked.

"No." Elyn said, remembering that once Dex had talked about them going to Maui, but the trip had fallen through at the last minute.

The kitchen seemed suddenly quiet.

"More coffee?" Elyn asked.

"No thanks. My plane leaves early in the morning, so I'm driving to San Francisco this afternoon, staying with friends overnight. They're expecting me for dinner so I better be going, but thanks, anyway."

He stood up, put on his jacket and zipped it.

At the door Elyn said, "Thanks for the wood, Doug. That was really good of you. Have a lovely trip."

He seemed to hesitate as though he wanted to say something more, then he moved to the top of the porch steps. There, he turned and said, "Well, take care, Elyn. And Merry Christmas."

"Same to you, Doug," she said over the surprising lump that rose suddenly into her throat. "Merry Christmas."

After watching Doug drive off, she went back inside and closed the door, thinking, Oh, yes, Merry Christmas.

Elyn went over to her drawing board and snapped on the radio. The plaintive voice of Judy Garland singing a holiday classic filled the room. All day Elyn had struggled with a sense of loneliness. Miss Thorne had left to spend a month with a cousin at the luxury Hotel del Coronado in San Diego, something she did every year. Ronnie was closing the shop to go to Lake Tahoe to join her family for a skiing holiday. Now Doug was leaving for Hawaii for yet another indefinite amount of time.

Slowly, Elyn realized this would be the first Christmas she would be entirely alone, without family or friends.

She felt a sort of sinking sensation verging on self-pity. Then determinedly she sharpened her stick of charcoal and tacked a sheet of sketch paper to her drawing board to work.

Pull yourself together. Stop feeling sorry for yourself.

Instead of feeling sad, she should count her blessings. She had kind friends, a roof over her head, food on the table, money in the bank. She had a lot to be thankful for. A great deal more than another young expectant mother had two thousand years ago! Neither did she have to ride forty miles on a donkey while nine months pregnant!

Chapter Fourteen

Elyn woke to another gray December morning. She peered out the rain-streaked kitchen window at the gloomy landscape. Well, she might as well hole up for the day. No reason to brave the storm. No need to go shopping. She had plenty of groceries—canned soup, bread, eggs, milk. To say nothing of the contents of the gift basket from Hawaii delivered on Christmas Eve. She still hadn't eaten half of the snack crackers, candied fruit, pineapple sweet bread, jars of preserves, jellies and macadamia nuts.

The card had read, "Christmas greetings from the Big Island. 'Mele Kalikamaka' Aloha. Doug Stevens."

Yes, this would be a good day to work. No distractions, no temptations to go out. She assembled her drawing materials and got to work on her sample Sophisticats cards.

The mild pains began late in the afternoon. They were so minor that at first Elyn dismissed them as the discomfort of late pregnancy.

But as the evening set in and the pains progressed, Elyn grew more anxious. The baby wasn't due for several more days. Elyn got out her book on childbirth and read the chapter on labor. Maybe. Could this be *it? Really it?* Elyn sincerely hoped not.

Ronnie had promised she would be with her at the first signs of labor, assured her that when the time came she would go with Elyn to the hospital. But Ronnie was still with her family on their skiing vacation in Lake Tahoe.

Suddenly it occurred to Elyn that she had no one to call, no one to accompany her to the hospital. If only she had attended Lamaze classes. Even if she had been sure she wanted natural childbirth, she had no one to ask to be her partner.

No, that wasn't true. Ronnie would have been wonderful. And there was always Doug.... But it was too late to think of that now. She would have to go through this entirely alone.

By eight o'clock the pains were steady and regular, impossible to ignore. Elyn went to the window and looked out at the dark night.

This had been the worst winter in the Valley for forty years. Everyone said so. Elyn turned on the porch light. She saw a layer of frost glistening in icy puddles on the driveway.

She shivered a little. She better not delay any longer. She needed to get herself to the hospital.

Her bag was mostly packed. She tossed in her brush, comb and toiletries. As she closed the bag, another pain gripped her. She had to hold on to the foot of the bed until it passed.

She took a long, shaky breath, then put on her coat, grabbed her handbag and took a last look around the little house. Next time she saw it, she would be bringing her baby home. Excitement mixed with panic.

Outside, Elyn carefully maneuvered the porch steps and the walk to her car. Stars glittered in the dark sky and the icy air was still. She stowed her bag and cosmetic case in the trunk, then squeezed herself under the wheel. With a hand that shook she inserted the key in the ignition. "Please, God, let the engine start."

It made a grinding sound, turned over protestingly a few times, then she shifted into first gear and released the clutch. "Okay, we're off. Thank you, God."

The drive along the winding road seemed endless. Finally, Elyn saw the neon hospital sign glowing eerily through a veil of mist. She pulled into the parking lot marked Patients and found a space just as another pain hit. She braked, breathing hard, and waited until the contraction was over before getting out of the car. She quickly collected her bags, then walked toward the entrance.

The lobby was quiet. At the information desk she gave her obstetrician's name to the clerk behind the counter, then took the clipboard she was handed.

"Just fill this out," the woman said. "We'll notify Dr. Alers you're here. Is anyone with you?"

Elyn shook her head. "No."

The clerk looked over Elyn's shoulder as if Elyn might be lying. She knew what the woman was thinking. Surely someone had accompanied a woman in labor, right?

"Well, somebody from Maternity will come down for you," the woman finally said.

Elyn sat down gingerly on one of the chrome-and-plastic chairs lining the waiting room wall. She fumbled in her handbag for her wallet to get out her insurance card to fill in the blanks on the patient admittance sheet. Suddenly a pain swept over her, leaving her dazed, shaky. This time the pain lasted a little longer than before. Elyn looked around desperately. She hoped someone came soon to take her wherever people who knew what to do were. She felt scared and terribly alone. She searched her mind for a prayer. All she could come up with was "His mercy endureth forever."

Finally a green-clad female wearing white running shoes appeared trundling a wheelchair down the hall. A nurse? The woman stopped at the admissions desk. The clerk pointed to Elyn.

"You're the one about to do the honors?" the woman said as she approached Elyn. "Well, we'll take you upstairs and get you prepped. Has your doctor been called?"

Before Elyn could answer, a sharp pain struck. She gasped and clung to the arms of the plastic chair. Her purse and the clipboard slipped out of her lap and onto the floor.

"Uh-oh, we better hurry." The woman helped Elyn

into the wheelchair, then pushed it down the corridor. "Who's your doctor?"

Elyn barely remembered saying "Dr. Alers" before being whisked into the elevator.

The next few hours were a blur. Elyn vaguely registered the glaring lights in the delivery room, the soothing voice of Dr. Alers encouraging her, the unbelievable pain, the blessed relief when the anesthetic took hold, then the faraway sound of a baby's cry.

"You've got a fine little boy, Elyn," the doctor said, her voice barely registering as Elyn drifted into unconsciousness, "and he's perfect...."

When Elyn finally opened her eyes, everything was quiet. She lay immobile, tucked tightly into a high bed in a room with pale-green walls. Louvered blinds shut out all but the narrow lines of dim light seeping through the slats. Elyn had no idea what time it might be.

She slid her hands down her body. She must have had the baby. She tried to sit up, but felt bruised and sore. Her mouth was dry, her throat parched. She groped for the call bell and pressed it.

A few minutes later the door opened. A shaft of bright light spilled into the room, a woman's figure outlined against it. "Awake, are you?" a voice asked. "Want to see your little fellow?"

"Oh, yes." To her own ears Elyn sounded hoarse.

"Just a sec and I'll go to the nursery and get him."

Elyn's heart was beating so loud, she could hear it pounding in her ears. At last the nurse returned carrying a small bundle. All Elyn could see was a tiny knitted cap sticking out from the corner of the blue blanket. The nurse came over to the bed.

"He's adorable. Wait till his daddy sees him. I bet he'll be proud."

Elyn hesitated. She might as well get used to telling people the truth.

"He won't see him," she said quietly. "I'm not married."

"Oh, gosh! I—I just came on duty. I didn't see your chart," the nurse stammered. "Sorry."

"Don't be. It's really better this way," Elyn said, and held out her arms for the baby.

She looked down into her baby's face. He was real, this small person who had been strangely unreal all these months. Now he was here in person. A part of her, yet something very much apart. He had taken his place in the universe. She took one of his tiny hands, examining each finger, one by one. She was in awe. He stirred, made little mewing sounds. He was so warm, precious, alive. Someday, most assuredly, he would grow up to tower over her with long legs, broad shoulders. But now he lay in her arms, belonging completely to her. She would treasure this moment, cherish it, keep it in her heart forever.

She had decided on the name Daniel. "We're going to be all right, Danny boy," she whispered softly while she cuddled him. "You and me, we're going to do just fine, I promise."

PART II

Chapter Fifteen

Doug was on the freeway heading back to Napa from San Francisco. Foggy mist was beading his windshield. He hadn't driven in this kind of weather in quite a while. Strange, after three months of sunshine in Hawaii. The remodeling job he'd done for his parents had taken longer than he'd anticipated.

He glanced down on the seat beside him at the plastic bag containing two leis. One was of creamy plumeria blossoms, the other pink carnations mixed with baby orchids. In Kona he had had a hard time deciding which one to choose to bring back to Elyn. In the end he bought both.

On the steering wheel his fingers tapped to the country-and-western tune playing on the stereo. He had never been this anxious to get back from the islands. A few times he had almost considered going into business in Hawaii. There were plenty of opportunities for a builder. Wealthy mainlanders wanting vacation homes.

But it had its drawbacks. It would mean catering to the sometimes erratic whims of clients. He was too independent to comply to ideas he didn't agree with. That was one of his shortcomings. Among others. Speaking out, being too blunt, saying what he thought. He winced, remembering how he'd gotten off on the wrong foot with Elyn Ross. Something he definitely didn't want to repeat. Something he hoped he could make right.

The image of Elyn's face came into his mind. He remembered that last afternoon before he left for Hawaii when he'd stopped by with the wood. There was something about her he had not seen before. Her summer tan had faded and the creaminess of her skin had made her long-lashed eyes look darker, larger, with a dreamy quality about them. She had a gesture of tucking her fair hair behind her ears that he'd found somehow childlike and endearing. Her softly curved mouth— Well, it was a mouth that, given the chance, he would like to kiss—

Doug struck his fist on the steering wheel. For being so fragile-looking, she was so brave. She had steel in those tiny bones.

What kind of guy would have let a woman like her go? Must have been out of his mind.

She'd had the baby by now. He had been tempted to call Elyn, but he resisted the urge. He knew this was a special time for mother and child, and he wasn't sure where *he* fit in. If at all. He might have called Ronnie, but in the end he'd decided against that, too. He would get the answers to all his questions when he saw Elyn again.

He wondered whether she'd had a boy or a girl. She probably wanted a girl. Women usually did. They liked to dress them in ruffly bonnets and dresses—that sort of thing. If it turned out to be a boy, that would be kind of hard for a single mom. He wondered if Elyn had any experience with boys. Any brothers? She hadn't said anything about having a family. He'd like to help out in some way. That is, if she'd let him.

Doug took the Napa off-ramp. He kept thinking about that gray December afternoon when he'd left Elyn. She'd looked so little, so vulnerable, he'd almost turned around and gone back. Canceled his trip. He remembered her expression as he'd said goodbye and wished her a Merry Christmas. Her soft lower lip had trembled a little and there had been such a lost look in her eyes....

He thought of that pathetic little tree she'd had. Wondered if she'd ever gotten around to decorating it?

Had she spent the holidays entirely alone? She said she had plans, but he hadn't quite believed her. He knew Lark Thorne had gone for her annual visit with her cousin in San Diego. He'd driven her into San Francisco to catch her plane. And Ronnie had gone away, too. He'd passed The Crow's Nest on his way out of town. A sign on the door had read Gone Skiing. Merry Christmas to All!

Doug glanced again at the flowers. He hoped he hadn't gone overboard. He'd also bought a big, plush teddy bear at one of the airport gift shops. And then there was the matter of the quilt.

When his mother had asked her usual not-too-subtle question about anyone special in his life, Doug had found himself telling her about Elyn. His mother had listened sympathetically. When he was getting ready to leave, she had given him a package.

"I want you to give this to your friend for her baby. I've become fascinated with Hawaiian quilts since we've lived over here. This is a crib-size one. The missionaries taught the Hawaiian ladies how to quilt, but the Hawaiians had their very individual interpretations. They made up their own patterns using symbols representative of the islands, the native fruits and flowers. This one has little geckos on it, those tiny lizards you see here."

"Oh, Mom, I don't know...." Doug had been doubtful. But his mother insisted, so he had packed the quilt with his things. Would Elyn think it too personal a gift? He wasn't sure. He'd have to play it by ear.

He hoped he hadn't given his mother the idea that there was anything serious going on between him and Elyn. He knew his mother worried about his bachelor status. She longed for him to find the right woman, settle down and be happy. She especially wanted grandchildren to brag about. Was she reading between the lines? Seeing more to what he'd told her about Elyn than what was actually there?

At the Calistoga intersection Doug had to stop for the red traffic light. He felt a strange impatience. He'd been away too long. Anything could have happened. He felt a leap of alarm. Elyn could have moved away.

The light flashed to green. He drove through town, not stopping at his own place. A ridiculous excitement gripped him. He couldn't wait to see Elyn, to see if everything was okay. An unreasonable sort of hope surged inside him as he closed the distance to Elyn's house.

When Elyn opened the door, for a minute Doug was speechless. She looked so different. Her hair now curved around her face just below her ears. She was wearing a ribbed tan turtleneck and faded blue jeans. It was the first time he'd seen her in anything but a paint-daubed smock or an oversize shirt. He hadn't realized she was so small and slim.

She gazed at him as though he'd suddenly dropped in from Mars. He managed to say, "Hi, how're you doing?"

"Fine, just fine. How was Hawaii?"

"Fine, great." He kept standing there, feeling foolish with the teddy bear under his arm, holding the leis and the other package. Finally, he thrust the plastic bag containing the leis at her. "For you."

"Why, Doug, how nice of you."

"I wasn't sure what kind you'd like. What your favorites are. They had so many."

"These are beautiful. Thank you."

He handed her the teddy. "This is for..."

She shifted the leis and took the stuffed animal. "Danny. I called him Daniel." Then she said, "Come in, please. Would you like to see the baby?"

"Sure would."

"I'll get him." She walked quickly into the bedroom.

He stood in the living room, waiting. He looked around and recognized the basket he had ordered sent to her at Christmas. It now held two blooming African violets.

"Here he is," Elyn said gently as she returned carrying a tiny blanket-wrapped bundle. "Danny meet Doug."

Doug swallowed. Babies had never seemed anything special. But now as he looked down into the small round face of Elyn's son, he felt a rush of emotion like nothing he'd ever felt before. He reached out a hand tentatively and the baby took hold of his finger. Doug looked at Elyn and grinned. "Hey, this fella's got quite a grip."

She smiled shyly. "Yes, he's very strong. Growing every day. Would you like to hold him?"

"Could I?"

"I'm about to give him his bottle. You could sit in the rocker while I warm it."

"Great." He held out his arms and Elyn transferred the baby to him. Doug walked carefully into the kitchen after Elyn. "How is the rocker?"

"Believe me, it's gotten lots of use. Especially the first few weeks. Until we got used to each other, he did a lot of fussing. Rocking him works like a charm." She got the formula bottle out of the refrigerator and placed it in a small saucepan on the stove, then turned the flame to low. "By the way, thanks, I really appreciated having it."

A few minutes later Elyn turned from the stove, the warmed bottle in hand. "Do you want me to take him now, or do you want to give the bottle to him?"

"He seems pretty comfortable. Let me try, okay?"

Elyn watched as Danny's little hands wrapped around the bottle and he made small slurping sounds. Doug looked at Elyn and smiled. "Seems okay." Then he suggested, "Why don't you open the other package? It's from my mother."

Elyn looked surprised. "Did you tell her about me?"

"A little. Just that we were friends. I hope that's true, Elyn."

"Of course." She paused. "I meant, did you tell her about...my situation?"

"Actually, I don't know much about it."

"That I'm raising Danny on my own?"

"She'd understand that. My older brother was born when my dad was in Vietnam. She was all by herself. She'd have nothing but sympathy and admiration for what you're doing."

Elyn smiled slightly. "That's a little different. Danny's father's never going to be in his life."

They were silent while Elyn undid the package and lifted out the quilt. "Oh, Doug, it's lovely. You must give me your mother's address so I can write her a thank-you note.''

''I will,'' he said as they gazed at each other for a long moment. ''I think he's finished.'' Doug held up the almost empty bottle. ''Boy, he can really put it down.''

''I know. Here, I'll take him, put him to sleep.''

Elyn disappeared with the baby into the nursery. While she was gone, Doug stood up and moved over to the door of the studio.

When Elyn returned, she said, ''Out like a light. He's such a good baby. Eats, sleeps—all on schedule. I'm so lucky.''

''Been doing any painting?''

''Not much. But I'm getting back to it. I'm working on a new project.''

''Besides Danny?'' he teased.

''Besides Danny. However, I did do a design for a baby announcement card that I sold. I find I can sketch him when he's sleeping.''

''I'm glad things are going so well for you, Elyn. I thought about you a great deal while I was away, hoped things were working out.''

''Thank you and thanks for all the nice presents.''

He moved toward the front door. ''Maybe I could stop by now and then. Teach Danny how to pitch and catch a fly ball.''

She laughed. ''I hope you won't wait that long. Sure, come anytime.''

"Well, I'll be on my way. I'm going up to see Lark. She okay?"

"Yes, she's doing wonderfully well. She loves the baby. I take him up there every day or so and she enjoys it."

"Neighbors are important. You both have good ones."

"So are friends. Thanks again, Doug, for everything."

An hour later Doug was on the road again, heading for his own house. He would have liked to stay longer at Elyn's, but he didn't want to overdo it, though she seemed to mean it when she said he could come by "anytime."

But she *had* seemed a little uncomfortable about the gifts. Especially the one from his mother. She'd said she loved it, mentioned how beautifully made it was, asked about the geckos. Still, he couldn't help think that she didn't like the idea of a stranger knowing so much about her.

Much as he longed to get to know her better, Doug did not want to overplay his hand. Elyn was such a private person. He sensed the unexpected gifts might have been too much. He didn't want to scare her.

He had a long way to go to convince her that they might have a future together.

Chapter Sixteen

Whenever Elyn thought of the early months of Danny's life, she was reminded of the device used in old movies to show the passage of time. Pages of a calendar blowing off into the wind one after the other.

During the first few weeks, day merged into night, night into day. And day became a marathon of preparing formula, feeding, diapering, bathing, rocking, laundering, then the whole routine was repeated the next day. She couldn't remember when she'd had a full night's sleep. Neither could she remember ever being so blissfully happy. Happy, but always tired. In fact, she'd had no idea a little baby could take up so much of her day. It had been difficult, but so very rewarding. Danny had been such a joy, given her back everything she'd expended on him. It had also been a time of healing and recovery. Dex's betrayal and her family's indifference had created a deep wound. Scar tissue had formed, thanks to three special people.

During these past months Elyn realized how important her friends were and how blessed she was to have such good ones. She didn't know how she would have survived single motherhood without their help, support and encouragement.

Ronnie, with her enthusiasm, her optimism, her can-do attitude, had literally picked Elyn up and shoved her in the right direction. And Lark, who treated her and Danny as if they were the child and grandchild she'd never had. Lark had even insisted Elyn use the heirloom cradle that had been in her family for generations.

Most surprising of all was her friendship with Doug. She recalled how she had rather disliked him at first, mistaking his self-assurance for arrogance, his generosity for pushiness. That image had totally changed.

With Danny he showed an unexpected tenderness that both surprised and touched her.

The fact that he seemed to take her and Danny under his wing puzzled her. Yet he showed the same protectiveness toward Miss Thorne. He was always checking on her, bringing her things, doing odd jobs for her without being asked. Why?

Admittedly Elyn knew very little about Doug other than he owned his own construction company, and obviously loved his parents. Why wasn't he married? she wondered. Good-looking, successful, great personality—she would have thought some woman would have snapped him up by now. Or maybe he had been. Maybe he had as complicated a past as she did.

Besides having Danny and nurturing good friendships, other aspects of her life were also coming together. She continued to sell some of her more traditional designs to two greeting card companies. For the time being she had put aside her work on the Sophisticats. When Danny was a little older, she could schedule uninterrupted time to work on that idea.

She had also sold a few of her paintings, thanks to Ronnie who, unknown to Elyn, had entered them in the silent art auction at that year's Mustard Festival gala.

She remembered vividly when Ronnie had told her of the sale, and how excited her friend had been.

"Elyn, I have such great news to tell you. Two of your paintings sold for top dollar at the art auction!"

"*My* paintings?"

"Yes. I didn't tell you because I knew you'd protest. But two of the ones I took to frame, I placed in the silent auction and they sold. I told you that you were good. Now this proves it."

Astonished, Elyn asked, "Which ones?"

"The one you painted in Golden Gate Park of the moon bridge and the one of the yellow Victorian house. And guess who bought that one?"

"How could I? Who?"

"Doug."

"Doug Stevens?"

"What other Doug do you know?" Ronnie demanded. "Of course, Doug Stevens! He said it looked like his grandparents' house in Marion, Ohio. He even pointed to the window of the second floor bedroom where he and his cousin used to sleep on summer visits. They used to crawl out early in the morning, slide down the roof, shimmy down the drainpipe to go fishing or swimming early in the morning. Isn't that a coincidence?''

Elyn was silent for a full minute, then she said slowly, ''That's so strange, Ronnie. That house isn't real. It's a figment of my imagination. I mean, I used some parts of real houses in San Francisco that I'd sketched, but I combined them and created that house. It's a pretend house. I thought of it as everybody's ideal of a home.'' Her voice trailed off dreamily. ''While I was painting it, I imagined the perfect family that lived there....''

''Well, whatever. Doug really liked it. Carried it home with him after writing the check without blinking an eye. The price was hefty, to say the least. They always start high at these events because it's for a good cause. I can't say exactly how much. Doug kept bidding on it and finally the other bidders fell away. The main point is, Elyn, you've got to start believing in yourself as an artist. You've got a talent, a God-given talent.''

Elyn felt humble. And curious. It seemed strange that her imagination and his reality had merged. She wondered if Doug would say anything to her about buying her painting. Or should she bring up the subject herself when next she saw him?

Unfortunately the opportunity did not present itself very soon. Doug was out of town most of that spring and summer, working on a new project. Though nobody saw much of him during those months, he kept in constant communication with Elyn, always inquiring about Danny.

One day in early September Doug showed up at the cottage. Danny was teething and fussy and Elyn was nearly at her wits' end. She had given up any idea of working. Nothing seemed to soothe or amuse him. She had walked him, rocked him and sung to him, but nothing had comforted him.

Suddenly she heard a vehicle come to a stop outside. She looked out the window and saw Doug coming up the porch steps carrying his toolbox. After a brief rat-a-tat knock he entered the house.

"Hi, Elyn. Hiya, fella!" he said to Danny, who immediately started smiling. Doug swung him up and tossed him in the air, causing Danny to gurgle with delight.

"Why, Doug, what are you doing here? I thought you were building a house in Ukiah."

"Waiting for a shipment of roofing tiles. Work halted until it comes." He tousled Danny's hair affectionately. "So, I figured I'd come over here and do a job."

"Lark didn't say anything about having anything done here."

"I didn't ask her. I just figured it was about time to baby proof the house. Get rid of things that might be dangerous when Danny starts walking."

"But he hasn't even taken a first step, Doug."

"Won't be long. Then he'll be into everything. So Be Prepared is my motto."

"A real Boy Scout, right?"

"As a matter of fact, yes." Doug grinned and handed Danny over to her. "It's very simple. I can do it in no time flat." He pointed to the lower cabinets in the kitchen. "They all need to be fixed so he can't open them easily and get into cleaning stuff, cleansers, that sort of thing. All your electrical outlets need plastic covers on them. Then I thought you'd need a gate across your studio entrance. That way you can work at your drawing table and still watch him in here, but he can't get into your paints and brushes."

"Why, Doug, that's very thoughtful of you. I should have thought of those things myself. I just didn't. Thank you."

"No problem," Doug said. "I'll get started. Where's the best place to begin?"

"I was going to give him a snack, so I'll put him in his high chair and he can watch you work in the kitchen. He'll love that."

It was interesting to see how professionally Doug went about his job. Elyn always admired people who were good at what they did, and Doug was one of them. He worked quickly and smoothly and had the cabinets done in no time. He went through the rest of the house, covering the electric sockets at floor level with small plastic discs. The gate across the door to the studio took a little longer. When he was finished, it was nearly five o'clock and Elyn decided the least she could do was ask him to stay for dinner.

Doug looked surprised. "You're sure? Won't it be too much trouble?"

"Of course I'm sure."

His eyes held a glint of mischief. "Spending more time in the kitchen these days, are you?"

Elyn had to laugh, recalling their exchange on this subject on one of their first meetings.

She turned back to Danny and fed him the last spoonful of applesauce, noticing that the baby was worn-out, his eyes already drooping. She excused herself to put him to bed, then returned to serve the meal.

"This is great, really delicious, Elyn," Doug said as she sliced him another piece of meat loaf.

"Wait until I serve dessert," she teased. "Apple crisp."

"I'm impressed."

"Don't be," she said. "Truthfully, this isn't my regular menu. I'm showing off." She got up and walked over to one of the kitchen cabinets, took a box off the shelf, then set it on the table so Doug could see it.

He looked puzzled. "Oatmeal? So what?"

"Haven't you ever read the label on an oatmeal box? It has three recipes printed on it. Meat loaf, apple crisp and oatmeal cookies. Tonight's menu!"

Doug nodded, then very seriously asked, "So where are the cookies?"

"You're impossible," she declared with mock indignation. "Not satisfied with two out of three?" She brought a ceramic cookie jar from the counter and plunked it on the table. "Help yourself." Then she poured them each a mug of coffee and sat down.

"So, how are things going in the greeting card business?" Doug asked after munching on a cookie.

"It's slow but steady. I haven't yet been able to figure out an achievable work schedule. Danny has to come first."

"That's important." Doug nodded.

For the next hour they talked easily about Danny, Lark, the house Doug was building.

"It's for a man from San Francisco. Probably a millionaire. At least money's no object. The architect comes out to the building site every other day with changes his client wants. Way over the estimated cost. Seems wealthy San Franciscans like the idea of having a place in Napa Valley. A vineyard and winery, possibly."

Elyn was surprised at how comfortable she felt with Doug that evening. Somehow he'd managed to make her hopeful again after the betrayal she'd suffered at the hands of Dex.

When Doug said he had to leave, Elyn walked to the door with him and finally got the courage to ask him about the painting he'd bought. She told him the house was make-believe.

His smile was slow, and something curious flickered in his eyes as he regarded her. "Well, maybe that just goes to show that our ideas of a home aren't too far apart.''

In the days and months that followed, Doug became more and more a part of their lives. Danny adored him. Whenever Doug stopped by, the little boy held up his arms to be lifted and tossed into the air. Elyn was grateful. She'd read in her parenting book that little boys needed male bonding. She appreciated Doug supplying what was so obviously lacking in Danny's life. A father. Whether Doug consciously filled that need or just loved Danny for himself, Elyn wasn't sure.

But she hoped to find out.

And she prayed for the courage to find out.

Chapter Seventeen

On a windy day in early February the bell over the door of The Crow's Nest rang as Elyn entered with Danny.

"Ronnie!" she called, looking around.

Ronnie appeared from the back of the store. She was dressed in a royal-blue twenties-style evening dress ablaze with sequins and fringed beading. She wore a glittering headband across her forehead from which fluttered two curled feathers. "So, what do you think?"

"Fabulous! But what's it all about?"

"This year's Mustard Festival gala has a twenties theme. Not that the twenties were so great for the wine industry, what with prohibition and all. Nostalgia stuff is very big and they want people to dress like characters out of *The Great Gatsby*. My vintage clothing business is doing fantastic. That's why I tucked this outfit away to wear myself."

"You look like something straight out of *Sunset Boulevard!*" exclaimed Elyn.

Ronnie came over to see Danny. "How is my little punkin? He gets cuter all the time, Elyn. By the way, you're welcome to look through some of my stock, pick out something *you'd* like to wear."

"*Me?* To the Mustard Festival gala? I'm not going."

"Why not? It would be good for you to get out, meet some people, make some connections—"

"No, I couldn't possibly. I couldn't leave Danny."

"We could get a sitter I know plenty of people—"

"Believe me, Ronnie, I'm not ready."

"Well, *next* year for sure."

Just then the bell over the door jangled again and Doug walked in. "Hi, ladies," he greeted them. "I saw your car outside, Elyn, so I thought I'd come in to see if you'd like to go for coffee. You, too, Ronnie."

Ronnie looked shocked, tossed her head and went into her Miss Piggy imitation. "*Moi?* Take off in the middle of the afternoon?"

Doug laughed. "That's been known to happen."

"But what if somebody came in and wanted to buy something? Thanks, anyway. But you and Elyn go on."

Elyn hesitated. "I have some errands to do, and it's almost time for Danny's nap."

Ronnie raised her eyebrows. "He looks wide-awake to me."

"Come on, Elyn," Doug coaxed.

Elyn still hesitated. "I have a package at the post office. I got a slip in my mailbox saying it was too big for the carrier to deliver."

"No problem," Doug said. "We can pick it up, put it in my truck and I'll take it out to the cottage for you."

"Won't that be too much trouble?"

"Not at all."

"Seems like you're always coming to my rescue."

Doug grinned. "Just call me a knight in shining armor."

"Be careful. I just might do that."

"Have fun, you two," Ronnie called after them as they left the shop.

They walked down the street to the small bakery and cafe. Inside smelled deliciously of fresh-ground coffee and pastries. The place was empty except for two elderly ladies at a window table. They took a table for four so Danny's carrying pack could be placed securely on one of the extra chairs.

A young, ponytailed waitress in a red-and-white striped T-shirt, blue jeans and a white apron greeted them to take their order. They chose cappuccinos and cranberry scones.

Seated across from Elyn, Doug thought how pretty she was. Funny, how much prettier she looked every time he saw her. Today her cheeks were rosy, her eyes sparkling, and she was wearing a knitted red beret that made her look like a schoolgirl.

"I take it Ronnie was modeling her costume for the Mustard Festival gala? Are you going?"

"No, are you?"

"I'll probably put in an appearance. They're kind of

fun." He paused. "Any particular reason why you aren't?"

"Do I need a reason?" Elyn raised her eyebrows. "If I do, Danny's a good enough one. I don't want to leave him. Not yet."

He nodded. The waitress brought their coffee and left. As they sipped their coffee and munched on their scones they slid into the easy camaraderie that increasingly had come to define their relationship.

Danny began to fuss, and Elyn slipped her jacket on and stood up. "This young man's getting sleepy. I didn't expect to be gone this long. I'll have to get him home."

"I'll carry him," Doug offered. He lifted the baby and tucked him into one arm. At the cash register the two white-haired ladies were getting their change, but stopped to ooh and ah at Danny. One said to Doug, "Your baby is darling."

"Thank you," Doug replied nonchalantly, handing the check to the cashier.

Elyn was amused. Of course the ladies had taken them for a family. She felt a sudden pinch of regret. The feeling she always got when she saw a young couple with a little child. She longed to give Danny that security of belonging to two people in love.

But she'd been betrayed once by a man who'd said he loved her. She couldn't afford to suffer another betrayal now—not with Danny in the equation.

Doug walked with her to her car and put Danny into the car seat, buckling him in carefully. "Give me your package slip. I'll bring out your delivery as soon as possible.''

"Thanks," Elyn said, thinking again how Doug had come to be her knight in shining armor.

But could he slay all her dragons...especially the ghosts of her past?

Chapter Eighteen

At two years of age Danny was a sturdy, active child who kept Elyn busy. He was also a very handsome little boy. It was because of her justifiable pride in him that Elyn learned a bitter lesson.

Impulsively she had sent pictures of Danny to her grandmother and her aunt Pat. Surely seeing him would make them want to be a part of his life.

Of course, as soon as she mailed the pictures, she had some misgivings. As it turned out, these were not misplaced. Weeks went by and there was no response. Finally a short, stiff note came from Grandma along with the returned pictures. "The boy looks like a healthy, happy child. But I wonder if he will thank you when he grows up. You have deprived him of a real family with two parents. I tried to tell you this, but you have always been stubborn. I fear you will live to regret your mistake."

Elyn tore up the note. What else could she have expected? She would always be on the sinner's bench as far as her grandmother was concerned.

The last line of the note had dealt the bitterest blow. ''I did not show these to your grandfather. He knows nothing about this.''

That seemed so cruel. Elyn imagined that her grandfather would love Danny. Who could resist him? But Elyn knew her grandmother too well to think she would ever change.

As for Aunt Pat, Elyn never heard from her. *She* didn't want to acknowledge Danny existed.

Whatever her family thought, Elyn knew she had done the right thing for *her*. She couldn't imagine a world without Danny.

The older Danny got and the more time she had to work on new designs, she hoped to increase her productivity. Already she'd received the good news that Sophisticats had been picked up. After a slow start, it seemed to be catching on now, and Elyn and Ronnie had hilarious sessions thinking up punch lines and captions.

Finally her life had settled into a pleasant rhythm.

Until a crisis threatened to change all that.

Elyn was awakened by the sound of Danny's fretful crying. She was up in a minute and raced into his room to find him coughing, a hoarse, croaking sound that struck terror into her heart.

She picked him up and felt his small body straining for breath. Oh, dear God, he's going to choke to death, he can't breathe. I've got to get him to the hospital right away, she decided desperately. Grabbing up a blanket, she wrapped him in it, shoved her feet into loafers, snatched her car keys and ran out into the foggy night.

When she reached the car, she strapped Danny into his car seat in the passenger seat beside her, propping him up with a pillow to ease the congestion. She rolled down the windows. It was freezing, but the damp, misty air floating into the car seemed to help Danny's breathing somewhat.

She didn't remember much about driving to the hospital. Her headlights made only fuzzy, yellow orbs in the fog-drenched night as she took the winding road at speeds she wouldn't have dared if it hadn't been such an emergency.

Oh, dear God, help us, Elyn prayed, tears rolling down her cheeks as she leaned forward. She gripped the steering wheel tightly so that her palms, sweaty with panic, would not slip. At last she saw the Emergency sign and swerved the car into a parking space.

A tall, dark-haired doctor was on call that night. "I'm Dr. Conti," he had told her before taking Danny from her. He hadn't even asked what the problem was; he was in control immediately.

When they were in the examination room, he said in a calm voice, "Looks like this little fellow has a bad case of croup. Well, we can fix that." He handled Danny quietly, quickly administering a shot to ease his breathing.

Relieved, Elyn began to cry, apologizing as she wiped her tears and searched in the pocket of her raincoat for a tissue. Dr. Conti pulled one out of a box on a nearby counter and handed it to her.

"I'm sorry." Elyn sniffled.

"Don't be. I'm sure you were very frightened."

He had been so reassuring, so kind. He had even walked out to the parking lot with her, helped her to get Danny comfortable in his car seat. "Feel free to bring Danny in if he doesn't feel better," he said. "But I'm sure he'll be just fine. Kids are remarkably resilient."

In recounting the whole episode to Ronnie a short while later, Elyn told her, "The most marvelous doctor took care of him. A Dr. Conti."

"Dr. Conti? Vin Conti? Tall, dark, handsome?" was Ronnie's awed exclamation. "You know who he is, don't you?"

Elyn shook her head, amazed at her friend's reaction.

"He's probably only about the most eligible bachelor in the entire Valley. You never heard of the Conti family? They're one of the oldest and most prominent wine-growing families in Napa Valley. They were among the very first to settle here from Italy and gained international fame for the quality of their product. Vin's father and older brother, Leo, manage the family business, leaving Vin free to pursue his medical career. He's only been back in the Valley a year or so after being associated with a prestigious medical group in the city."

Ronnie paused and looked serious. "Did he act interested in you? I mean, did he seem attracted?"

"Hardly." Elyn scoffed. "I had my raincoat on over my pj's, no makeup, hair uncombed—come on."

But Ronnie persisted.

"His mother is the one who started the Concerts in the Vineyards. She is the grande dame of society here. Knowing her son could be a great entrée to her."

"What do you mean?" Elyn asked, puzzled, then added, "I'm almost afraid to ask."

"One of my best customers is a member of the committee handling the promotion, publicity and advertising for the Concerts in the Vineyards this summer. She's admired your paintings and I told her you were also a bestselling greeting card designer—"

"You didn't!"

"Of course, I did. The point is, they'll be giving the commission for the artwork to someone, and it might as well be you. Anyway, she says Mrs. Conti is the one you need to show our design ideas to for this summer's series. If you're picked it means your design or logo will be used on the ads, the programs and everything else pertaining to the concert series. It's a wonderful opportunity, Elyn. That's *your* Dr. Conti's mother, by the way."

"He's not *my* Dr. Conti, Ronnie," Elyn corrected. "Besides, how would I contact her to present my work?"

Ronnie rummaged in her huge tote bag. "Here's my customer's telephone number. You can call her and set up an appointment with Mrs. Conti. But you better do it right away."

"But, Ronnie, I haven't a single idea for such a project."

"Well, pray about it." Ronnie gave her a beatific smile.

Doug was concerned when Ronnie told him about the episode with Danny and came rushing out to the cottage. With a peremptory knock, he entered the house and confronted Elyn. "Why didn't you call me? I would have come and taken you to the emergency room."

"There wasn't time, I didn't think. I guess I'm so used to doing things myself. I'm the only one really responsible for Danny and I can't be weak."

She didn't mean to sound pitiful or defensive, but since the night of the emergency it hit her anew how very alone she was.

"You certainly aren't weak, Elyn. You're one of the strongest people I know."

"That's why I try to do things on my own. I've learned people can fail you—"

"You can count on me, Elyn," Doug said, his mouth tightened in a stern line. "Not all men are like that heel who deserted you."

Whether it was a delayed reaction from her scary experience or just the relief of letting go, Elyn burst into tears.

Immediately Doug was beside her. He put his arms around her, pulling her close. "It's okay, Elyn, just let it all out. I know it must have been frightening."

Elyn leaned against the broad, hard strength of him,

allowing herself the luxury of feeling safe, protected. Slowly she drew away and wiped her eyes.

"It's just that if anything happened to Danny, I don't know what I'd do. Danny is all I have. I'm all he has."

"It doesn't have to be that way, Elyn. You have people who really care about you and Danny. You don't need to feel alone. You don't need to be alone."

Suddenly the mood between them changed. Doug seemed to be offering her something that she desperately wanted—needed—but still couldn't fully embrace.

She pulled back farther. "Sorry, I didn't mean to make a fool of myself."

"Nonsense. I bet it's been a long time since you let yourself cry."

Elyn gave a shaky laugh. "Not for quite a while. You just happened to be the unlucky bystander."

"Anytime," he said brusquely, his behavior now a little awkward.

He left soon afterwards, and Elyn felt strangely let down.

There had been such blessed relief in letting him hold her. Doug was so strong, so dependable, so steadfast, so utterly honest. A man she could trust with Danny, with herself, with their life. She could almost pretend that she had the right to linger in Doug's arms, safe, comforted, protected. If only it were possible.

But she had committed herself to another path. She couldn't let herself be dependent on him or anyone. She was in this situation alone and for the long haul. For Danny's sake, she had to be strong and to get stronger.

Chapter Nineteen

Elyn's third March in the Valley came in like a lamb instead of the proverbial lion, then April ushered in a beautiful spring and early summer.

On a warm June afternoon, Elyn and Ronnie sat in canvas arm chairs blowing iridescent bubbles from jars of liquid soap to the delight of Danny paddling happily in his plastic swimming pool. In contrast to the light-hearted gurgles of Danny as he tried to catch the soapy balls before they burst, their conversation had been a serious one.

Elyn sighed. "The real problem is, what am I going to tell Danny when he is old enough to ask questions?"

"Simple. Just tell him his father was a—"

"Ronnie!" Elyn remonstrated. "Don't! Danny's picking up every new word he hears now. We have to be careful what we say in front of him."

"You read too much of that psychobabble stuff. You know those books are probably written by people who never get near a child. There was this movie I saw about a child psychologist who actually detested children.''

"Oh, Ronnie, forget movies, I'm talking real life."

"Well, my advice is not to worry about it, Elyn. By the time Danny is old enough to ask questions, you'll probably be happily married and Danny will have a wonderful stepfather. Like Doug..."

"How many times have I told you, Ronnie, that I'm not interested in getting married? Or having any kind of serious relationship. Not now, maybe not ever."

"You're too young and attractive to say that, Elyn." Ronnie took a long breath and blew a series of bubbles directly at her. "What about Vin Conti?"

Elyn rolled her eyes. She wished she had never shared with Ronnie the incident with the doctor. "You've already told me what a prestigious family he's from, how his mother is the queen of Valley society. Can you imagine her reaction if he wanted to marry someone with the kind of baggage I have? The Conti name would be besmirched if her son, her pride and joy, was seriously interested in an unmarried woman with a child."

"Nobody thinks that way anymore, Elyn."

"I do. Regina Conti does and probably Vin does, too. For your information—" Elyn gave her friend a sly, superior glance "—not that it is any of your business, but since you make my marital prospects such an issue, I'll just say this. *If* I were interested in finding a stepfather for Danny, he'd have to meet pretty high standards."

"Well, what kind of man *would* suit your bill of requirements?"

Elyn took her time answering. She blew some bubbles in Danny's direction before saying, "A man I could trust absolutely, a man of integrity, a man who knows who he is and what he wants in his life. A strong man both morally as well as physically. A compassionate person, sensitive and gentle..."

The sound of a pickup coming up the drive made both of them turn. Doug braked, pulled to a stop and waved one tanned arm out the cab window.

"Speaking of which," Ronnie remarked.

"Ronnie! Behave," cautioned Elyn.

Doug got out of the truck, then leaned back inside. He brought out a red-and-white plastic cooler and walked toward the trio under the shade of the sprawling oak tree. "Hi, everyone."

"Doug! Doug!" Danny exclaimed.

"Ho, Danny boy! Whatcha doin', fella?" Doug squatted beside the pool, sitting on his heels. Danny squealed happily, splashed over to the side of the pool and held up his hands to be lifted. Doug swung him up in the air, causing Danny to scream with laughter.

Ronnie gave Elyn a significant look and raised her eyebrows.

Ignoring her, Elyn called to Doug, "Careful, Doug, he's dripping water. He'll get you soaking wet."

"Doesn't matter," Doug said, tossing Danny up again to the little boy's glee. "I brought you all something."

He set Danny down on the grass, patted him on the head. "Popsicles. What flavour do you want, old buddy?"

Doug opened the top of the cooler and handed Popsicles to Ronnie and Elyn, then let Danny point to the one he wanted. Doug undid the paper wrapper for him, placed both the boy's chubby little hands around the stick, then pulled Danny comfortably onto his knee. He glanced around. "Boy, what a deal—I'd like to take a dip myself."

"Help yourself," Elyn invited.

"Thanks anyway, but I'm going over to the lake on my way home. What I really stopped by for was to ask if you and Danny would like to go on a picnic Saturday." He turned to Ronnie. "You're welcome to come along, too, Ronnie."

"Thanks, but some people have to work," she said archly.

"Who's minding the store this afternoon then?" Doug countered.

"I have Luisa Ramirez working for me a few afternoons a week. She's earning money for college next year. And it gives me some time off. Which I deserve."

"Me, too," Doug commented. "I've been working ten-hour days on my project. I'm giving myself a day off, too. So, how about tomorrow, Elyn?"

"Yes, I'd love it." She made a point of avoiding Ronnie's I-told-you-so looks.

"This is my special, private picnic area," Doug told Elyn the next day as they took a turn off the highway and onto a rutted road that was hardly more than a wide path. Doug shifted to low gear. "I found this property a couple of years ago when I was looking for a building site. I decided to hold on to it so that some day I can build my own house on it."

A three-story Victorian? Elyn wondered, thinking of her painting Doug had bought.

He glanced over at her. "I think you'll like it. A wide creek runs through it. Right now it's a wonderful place for kids, shallow enough for Danny to play."

The road wound through towering trees and every time they hit a bump Danny would crow and clap his hands. At last they pulled into a shaded grove and came to a stop.

"Here we are," Doug announced as he braked. He jumped out and unbuckled Danny's seat belt and lifted him out of the truck. Blanket, picnic basket and cooler came next, followed by a bag of plastic boats and other water toys.

Elyn looked around in awe. "This is perfect, Doug."

"I hoped you'd like it." He smiled.

Danny could hardly wait to take off his sneakers and shirt and get in the water. Doug took him by the hand and led him down to wade.

The sunlight filtered through the willows that lined the bank warming the water. Danny played happily with the toy boats Doug had brought along for him, and Doug helped him to build a small dam with twigs and rocks to create a pool where Danny could float them and still stay safely in the shallow water.

Elyn stretched out on the blanket, watching the two of them. They made a picture, the kind featured in magazines about family values. Exactly the kind used to illustrate articles about parents spending more time with their children.

She felt her heart twist. From working in an advertising agency she had learned the tricks of producing those pictures. All posed by professional models. All artificially arranged to project a certain image.

She halted her cynical thoughts. Doug and Danny's relationship was real, warm, loving. What was wrong with the picture then?

If she had only met Doug years ago, before Dex, before... No use daydreaming. Their paths never would have crossed unless...she had come to Calistoga in the first place when she was running away from Dex, trying to run away from herself.

In spite of the warm sun on her back, Elyn shivered. She had promised herself not to look back, not to stir the old embers of regret.

"Hungry?" Doug asked, breaking in on her self-absorbed thoughts.

"Famished." She toweled Danny off and slipped a T-shirt over his head while Doug opened the wicker hamper and started setting out the hearty picnic he had insisted on providing—sliced ham, smoked turkey, crusty

French rolls, potato salad, cherry tomatoes, green grapes, brownies and a huge thermos of lemonade.

Afterward, a sleepy-eyed Danny, still clutching one of the little boats, consented to lie down for a nap and was soon fast asleep.

Doug moved over to sit beside Elyn. "That's a great boy you have, Elyn."

"I worry sometimes. You hear such terrible things about sons being reared alone by a doting mother. I don't want Danny to grow up with all sorts of complexes that I inadvertently caused."

"I wouldn't worry about that, Elyn. You're doing a fine job." Doug added, "Of course, you know it doesn't have to be that way. You don't have to feel you're completely alone. There are people more than willing to share raising Danny with you, Elyn." He paused. "Me, for instance."

Elyn stiffened slightly. She had not expected her casual comment to lead to this. She looked into Doug's eyes and what she saw there took her breath away. It was all there, so shining clear, there could be no mistake. Hope, love, longing. Possibility flowed through her. It was as though everything she had ever imagined could be hers was there waiting for her to claim.

A breathless moment passed. Then Doug leaned forward, placed one hand along her cheek and gently kissed her. It was a long, sweet kiss. There was tenderness in it, yet the promise of much more.

Slowly Elyn opened her eyes, then drew back out of his arms.

"Elyn, I've been wanting to do that for months. You must have guessed I've fallen in love with you."

"Please, don't say that, Doug. I thought you understood. I'm not ready for a relationship...not yet."

"Why not? What are you afraid of?"

What *wasn't* she afraid of? Having her heart broken? Betrayal, abandonment, losing herself. Instead she just said quietly, "I have all I can do with my career, with Danny. I can't take on anything else. Especially something as complicated as a relationship."

"Why does it have to be complicated? It's very simple. I love you. I love Danny. I didn't realize what was missing in my life until you and Danny came into it. I can't think of anything better than being with you two for the rest of my life. I know it would work out. That is, if you'd let it. Or are you too hung up on the past to take a chance on the future?"

She had never thought of it like that. Trust Doug to put it so directly. She didn't know how to answer him.

"Is that such a bad idea, Elyn? You, me, Danny—the three of us building a life together. A marriage based on mutual respect, love. I admire you so much, Elyn. Not just for what you've done with Danny, but for so many other things. Besides, you're beautiful, inside and out, and talented and—"

"Stop, Doug. I'm none of those things." She shook her head. "Some days I'm barely making it."

"It doesn't have to be like that, Elyn. That's what I'm trying to tell you. I want to be there for you, to help you with Danny and any other way I can."

"Doug, I don't want to hurt you, but it's out of the question. I'm just not able to make any kind of commitment."

Doug's jaw clenched. He started to say something else, then looking downcast said, "My fault. I thought you wanted the same things—love, building a home together. I took it for granted that you cared."

"I do care. You're a wonderful friend. One of the best friends I've ever had but—"

"Friendship might not be a bad basis for marriage."

"Yes, but it's not enough."

He reached for her hand, pressed it. "Okay. I didn't say it was *all* that mattered. Didn't you feel anything just now when we kissed?"

Elyn took a deep breath. Of course, she had. She had wanted Doug's kiss to go on and on. It had been a wonderful soaring feeling of happiness, something she hadn't felt in a very long time. Reality had penetrated just in time. Doug was not a man one could use just to satisfy the need to feel loved, desirable.

Elyn moved a little away from him. "Doug, can't you accept what I'm saying? Believe that I'm not ready?" She paused and continued sadly, "If you can't—then we'll have to stop seeing each other and that would be terrible for Danny."

Doug could not hide his disappointment. There was a

tense moment of silence, then he shrugged. "I wouldn't want that, Elyn." He gave a rueful smile. "Let's just say that kiss never happened. We can just go on as we have, okay?"

About then Danny woke up and the day went on. But Elyn knew things had subtly changed between her and Doug. Their relationship would never be quite the same again. Neither would their friendship. It was inevitably altered. The casual lightheartedness had been lost.

Chapter Twenty

A week went by, then two. Doug did not call or come by. Elyn found she missed him more than she could have imagined. Not for the first time, she wondered if she had damaged their friendship beyond repair. Even Lark remarked on his absence when Elyn was up at the big house one day visiting her.

"Doug hasn't been around in a while. Maybe he's off on one of his Good Samaritan trips."

Elyn looked at her questioningly.

"He works with Habitat for Humanity, building houses for poor, disabled people or others who can't afford housing. He goes two or three times a year sometimes, as far as Texas or Mississippi, to work for a few weeks. No pay, of course."

That was just like him, Elyn thought. Doug Stevens was a thoroughly decent guy, a truly good man. She had had many second thoughts after their ill-fated picnic, wondering if she had been too quick to discourage Doug.

For all his good qualities he was also proud. She doubted if he would repeat his proposal.

The following Sunday, when Lark asked Elyn to drive her to St. Luke's, Elyn never felt less like going to church. However, she had enrolled Danny in the Nursery Sunday School, as well as the day care program. He loved to go to "school," and not wanting to disappoint either him or Lark, Elyn found herself seated in a pew.

As usual, the interior was restfully dim with candle-light. At the sound of the organ, two well-scrubbed boys in starched white surplices and red cassocks preceded the minister down the center aisle and took their places at the altar. Unfamiliar with the hymnal, Elyn simply lis-tened to the voices around her raised in song. The quaintly worded ancient hymns were far different than those of her childhood church, yet still strangely sooth-ing.

The sermon, however, caught her attention and brought her fully alert.

"God has a plan and purpose for each of our lives. It is up to you to prayerfully seek it. His plan includes you becoming all that you can be. He wants you to have a rich, abundant life that is challenging and satisfying. He has given you certain individual gifts to lead the life He has designed for you.

"He has given us the means, the intelligence, the tal-ent to perform the tasks He has put us on this earth to do. In Proverbs 16:3, it is written, 'Commit your work to the Lord, then it will succeed.'

"All you must do is have faith and believe and He will bring it to pass. Faith as small as a mustard seed."

Elyn felt her whole body tingle. Surely, this was meant for her. This was exactly what she needed to hear. She had to be more trusting. Have faith and believe. It sounded simple enough, but could she do it?

As she drove home, Elyn was still caught up in the minister's message. She wanted to feel that she was living the life, doing the work He wanted. She kept turning over the words. All you need is faith as small as a mustard seed.

How could drawing silly little cats, writing one-line zingers on cards be committed to the Lord? It was too easy, and the end result too shallow. Maybe. Maybe not. People loved the cards, didn't they? The humorous quips made them smile, laugh even, and want to share them. Maybe the cards weren't serious, profound or terribly important, but wasn't her talent God's gift? The idea had come like one. Lark's cats, especially Esme, had been the inspiration. And that gave Lark immense pleasure. She also had to remember that the idea for Sophisticats had come to her when she was nearly bankrupt of ideas. Had come at a time when she desperately needed some way to make a steady income. Some way to work at home and take care of her baby.

She should do what the minister suggested, thank God for the artistic talent He had given her. Use it to give Him glory.

*   *   *

The next day, while Danny was at day care, Elyn went up to the mineral pool. She felt a sense of expectation inside. She'd felt it since the sermon yesterday. Something stirred within her. A feeling that something was about to be revealed to her. Something she was to learn or to do.

In the pool she let her mind drift just as her body was lifted and borne by the bubbling spring water. Pictures passed through her mind. The night before, she had sifted through some of the watercolors she had done since coming to the Valley. Scenes in early spring of the vineyards when the ground was covered with golden mustard blooms between the rows of grape stakes. Others were of later in the season when the leaves were a lush green as the grapes began to ripen. Now in full summer, the crop was coming into harvest, glistening clumps of grapes, amethyst, cedron and rich burgundy, their leaves gorgeous, scarlet-edged. A year's cycle told by nature. It was a miracle. Like the cycle of her own life.

A wave of gratitude swept through her. She was so grateful to have come to this beautiful part of the country, to have found a home, a real home for Danny and her, friends, and a sense of place. It had taken courage, which she didn't think she had. But most of all it had taken faith. Fragile as it was, she had nurtured it by prayer and Bible reading.

Faith as small as a mustard seed. She had read somewhere that mustard added some necessary nutrient to the soil to make the grapes better. Faith, even a little amount, gave a life its meaning.

Hers had been planted early and although neglected for years was now growing and getting stronger. Like the mustard seed, eventually she hoped it would grow stronger, hardier.

Mustard seed. The name kept repeating itself in her mind. Why not a line of inspirational cards? Mustard Seed! The idea sprang full-blown. Why not?

Sophisticats was doing well. They were repeating the designs and the one liners every few months. The demand continued. She only had to come up with six to ten new ones a year. Maybe this was what she needed. A new idea to reflect her newfound faith.

She had come to love Scripture, its lyric beauty, its strengthening quality. A verse for almost every occasion could be found in it. She could use some of her watercolors. She must have at least a half dozen usable ones already.

Excited now, Elyn got out of the pool and hurried back to the house. In her studio she looked up all her favorite Scripture verses, the ones that had particularly given her comfort, solace. She listed them. Then she looked through her portfolio, picking out the paintings that best illustrated that specific verse. Elyn's enthusiasm grew. She felt her adrenaline flow. It will work, I just know it will, she kept saying over and over.

For the next few days she worked feverishly. When she completed six designs she made slides. She also had them made into cards and did the Scripture verse on the inside in calligraphy.

In a cover letter to the publisher Elyn outlined all the possibilities where a gentle inspirational card would be appropriate. She didn't oversell her idea. She believed the cards would speak for themselves.

She also knew what one of the arguments against them might be. Since Sophisticats was doing so well, her editor might not want her to take time away from that popular line to start an entirely new and different style of card.

However, Elyn was convinced this was more than a clever idea. She felt truly inspired. All she asked was that they give this idea a chance to see what would happen.

With high hopes Elyn sent her packet off express mail with a prayer.

After this period of intense work, Elyn felt depleted. It was then she suddenly missed Doug terribly. He was always so interested in her work, liked to see her sketches, her new designs. She would have loved to share this exciting new concept with him.

Danny missed him, too. He often asked, "Where's Doug?" "Is Doug coming over?" She hadn't known what to answer. Maybe she had made a bad mistake, giving Doug such an ultimatum. Friendship or not, he was important in Danny's life. But maybe she had hurt Doug too much. For Danny's sake, she prayed the hurt she might have inflicted would heal.

Elyn had heard God did not always answer prayers the way expected, so she was surprised how hers was answered. She was just pulling out of a parking space downtown when she heard the familiar tap of Doug's horn. She glanced in her rearview mirror and saw his blue pickup. Within moments he was out of his truck and leaning in the window she had rolled down asking, "Can a fellow change his mind? I'm a slow learner, I guess, but I'm ready to accept your terms. I really miss you and Danny. How about if I bring a video out tonight and we watch a movie?"

"Sounds good."

"What's your pleasure? Drama, western, romance? Or horror?"

Elyn gave a mock shudder. "Not horror. A western, I think."

"Okay, see you later then?"

Elyn found herself smiling as she drove home. Doug was back in her life, and evidently with no hard feelings. She was looking forward to the evening. And she couldn't help but wonder again if this was an answer to her unspoken prayer.

Chapter Twenty-One

That fall was the happiest, most fulfilling time Elyn had experienced since coming to the Valley.

There was now a pattern to her day. Three mornings a week, Danny went happily off to the day care offered by St. Luke's Church. Those mornings Elyn used to work. She rarely had dark times anymore when thoughts of Dex depressed her. Danny was such a constant delight and gave her so much joy, she could only be thankful.

Doug had come back into their lives as casually and comfortably as though there had never been a break in their relationship. Without calling he would sometimes come by and pick up Danny to take him on an adventure of some kind for just the two of them. Other times he would just tell her, "You need a break," even if it was only so she could take a long bubble bath or just go to the grocery store by herself. "Go ahead, we'll be fine. We're great pals. And you need a break." Doug seemed to understand that being a single mother was a twenty-four-hour duty, with little time off.

Her life was good, and Elyn did not allow herself much time to look back with regret. What had happened had happened. She was blessed with all the things she had once thought out of reach.

To celebrate Danny's third birthday in December, Ellen gave a party. A small one—just Ronnie, Lark and Doug.

Elyn twisted streamers of crepe paper from the ceiling light and tied the ends in big bows on the backs of the four chairs around the kitchen table. There were colorful place mats and paper napkins.

Danny had been persuaded to lie down for a rest before their guests came. "Then you can stay up later," she had promised.

Ronnie planned to close her shop early, pick up the cake at the bakery and bring Lark. Just as Elyn was brushing Danny's hair, Ronnie and Lark arrived with gaily wrapped presents. Shortly afterward Doug showed up, carrying a large cardboard box.

"You may want to kill me, Elyn," he said as he set the box down on the floor. From inside came some strange scuffling and a squeak or two. "But before you object too much, let me say that it's my firm belief every boy should grow up with—"

"Oh, Doug, you didn't," Elyn gasped. "As if I didn't have enough to do with a small child!"

"Wait, hear me out." Doug held up a warning hand. "I ask these two ladies to be my witnesses to the following statement." He glanced first at Miss Thorne, then at Ronnie. "I solemnly promise to undertake the housebreaking and training, and within months you will have a wonderful house pet plus a watchdog, as well as a great companion for Danny." With that he opened the top of the box and lifted out an adorable, squirming, golden-haired puppy, whose tail was wagging like a metronome.

Elyn watched in helpless amusement as boy and dog fell in love with each other.

Doug turned to her with a sheepish expression. "Elyn, if you don't want it, I'll accept that. I'll take him home myself and keep him. He's the pick of the litter, although he is a mix—part golden retriever, part Irish setter. But he'll have a glorious color and a sweet disposition, I can guarantee that. I know both the mother dog and the male. They belong to a friend of mine."

By this time Danny was on the floor, the puppy was licking his cheek and ear with his little pink tongue and Danny was loving every minute of it.

"What can I say?" Elyn smiled helplessly. "Danny's already fallen in love with him."

Both Miss Thorne and Ronnie took turns holding and petting the puppy. His little pink tongue was busy giving them ecstatic kisses as Doug looked on like a proud godfather, watching as the puppy was passed from one adult to the other.

"I hope you don't mind too much, Elyn. I'll do the training and help Danny learn to take care of him. I'll build a doghouse for him, if that's okay with you, Miss Thorne?"

"I think it's wonderful for Elyn and Danny to have a dog. We always had at least three when I was growing up here. Puppies, too. If I didn't have the three cats, I'd be tempted to take this fellow myself."

"What shall we call him?" asked Elyn, knowing her question meant she had consented.

Suggestions were forthcoming, but none seemed right.

"He'll grow into his own name," Doug said. "I've seen that happen."

They fed the puppy some of the food Doug had brought along, then Doug and Danny took the puppy for a walk. When they returned, the puppy was put back in the box where he curled up and went promptly to sleep.

It was time to unwrap the rest of the presents. Ronnie and Lark had collaborated on their gift. From Lark came a picture book—*The Velveteen Rabbit*—and Ronnie had found the perfect velour floppy-eared bunny to go with it. The accompanying cards were opened and handed around for everyone to read.

After Elyn served the ice cream and cake, they realized it was getting dark outside and Danny was tired from all the excitement. Ronnie offered to take Lark home, and Doug bundled up the puppy in the box and started for the door.

"You really don't mind, do you, Elyn? I guess I took a lot for granted going ahead and bringing this pup. If you don't want—"

"Oh, Doug, I think it was a wonderful idea. I appreciate very much the way you think ahead about what Danny will want and need. I wouldn't have thought of it."

Doug grinned. "You mean it's a 'guy thing?'"

Elyn laughed. "You could say that. Anyway, thanks."

As Elyn tucked a sleepy Danny into bed that night, covering him with the Hawaiian quilt Doug's mother had given him, she felt a warm glow. It couldn't have been a happier day, a wonderful birthday for her little boy, surrounded by friends, a circle of love.

Elyn turned the night-light on and tiptoed out of the room. It was then that her gaze fell on a small wrapped package on the kitchen counter. A present for Danny that somehow had been overlooked?

But when she picked it up and examined it, the card read, "To the Best Mommy in the World." She opened the box and found enclosed a beautiful leather wallet with a tiny flashlight on the key chain. Inside was a picture of Danny. One she had never seen. Doug must have taken it on one of their outings.

Who but Doug would have thought of something like this?

Elyn was suddenly hit by a blinding truth. Doug was

so special. The kindest, most thoughtful friend she had ever had. More than that really...the "shining knight" she had kidded him about being. She thought of the numerous times, the countless ways he had been there for her, anticipating her needs, helping her out, actually "rescuing" her. Doug had all the qualities and values she had always admired.

She felt a pang of regret. Why hadn't she met someone like Doug earlier in her life? Certainly before she had been swept away by someone like Dex.

Chapter Twenty-Two

It had become a ritual that Friday evenings Ronnie came out to the cottage for supper and to spend the evening.

"Are you hungry?" Elyn asked her. She had made lasagna and just put it in the oven a few minutes before Ronnie arrived.

"Not too. I was on a diet, but I broke down about four and ate a taco. So I can wait. Whenever you're ready is fine. By the way, do you remember that customer I told you about, the one on the summer Vineyard concert series committee? In fact, I believe I gave you her card at some point. Anyway, she was in the store today and said she'll set up an appointment for you with Regina Conti about designing the logo. She really wants you to submit a proposal this year."

"Oh, Ronnie, I still don't have a clue for an idea."

"Well, get cracking. Those things are decided way ahead of time. So it's important you get in touch with her as soon as possible. Here is her telephone number again."

Elyn took the card and fastened it to the refrigerator with a butterfly magnet, then they sat down to eat.

"Now the next thing we have to decide is what you're going to wear to the Mustard Festival Gala this year," Ronnie said.

Her fork halfway to her mouth, Elyn looked at her friend. "Who said I was planning to go?"

"*This* year, you are. No excuses. I insist. It will be fun, Elyn. It will be a good place to meet people, make some contacts."

"Oh, Ronnie, I don't know."

"Now, Elyn, don't be stubborn. It's business. It's called networking. A must for someone trying to establish a career. Think of it as building a future for Danny!"

"That's just it. Who would take care of Danny? I've never left him with a sitter."

"I know the perfect person. A really responsible teenager who helps me in the shop on weekends. She's an A-student, a senior at the high school, and the oldest in a family of five. She takes care of her younger brothers and sisters all the time, plus she's going to study nursing next year when she graduates. What could be better? Her name is Luisa Ramirez. I'll arrange it. I'll also dig up something gorgeous and glamorous for you to wear."

In the end, Elyn agreed to go.

They spent the rest of the evening chatting about numerous things, and as usual exchanged some possible quips for Elyn's Sophisticats cards. Elyn started to tell Ronnie about her new Mustard Seed line proposal, but since she hadn't heard from the greeting card company yet, she decided not to say anything.

As Ronnie got ready to leave she told Elyn, "I've already recommended you for next year's Mustard Festival artwork. That's a commission that's always up for grabs, open to artists all over the Valley. People love my new logo and my cards, and I always tell them who did them."

"Oh, Ronnie, you're such a good friend."

At the front door Ronnie asked, "How's Doug? I haven't seen him around lately." She gave Elyn a knowing look. "But I guess you have."

"He stops by now and then to see Danny," Elyn replied non-committally.

"Sure. To see Danny." She raised her eyebrows. "Of course."

"Now don't start that, Ronnie. Doug is just a good friend."

"Oh, yes, I know. The thing is, he'd like to be more. Don't you see that, Elyn?"

"No, I don't. Doug and I understand each other. He's just a very good friend."

"Have you asked Doug lately to define your friendship? Personally, I think he'd have a very different definition."

"Ronnie, you are so wrong!"

"No, it's *you* who are wrong, Elyn."

After Ronnie was gone, Elyn kept thinking of what her friend had said. Not by a word or gesture had Doug broken their agreement. Again, she had to wonder if she was expecting too much.

Elyn went out to the kitchen to straighten up. As she passed the refrigerator, she saw the business card Ronnie had given her. She would call the woman tomorrow. Ronnie was right. It was a great opportunity. She would take her friend's advice.

At least on that.

The next day, Elyn called the woman to set up an appointment to meet with Regina Conti. It was arranged that Elyn would go to Mrs. Conti's home to present the sketches of her ideas for the concert logo.

In the ten days leading up to her interview, Elyn worked feverishly on two possible designs. Ronnie agreed with Elyn that the stylized silhouette of a violin and cello angled against a background of a musical score was the best. The design was in black and white, stark but effective.

Although Ronnie had raved about her sketches and Elyn had rehearsed her presentation to perfection, on the day of her appointment Elyn felt very nervous.

She drove up the winding gravel driveway to Casa Conti. Ronnie had briefed her a little on what to expect, but Elyn's first glimpse of the mansion was daunting. The house was a castlelike structure of stone, with turrets and towers and stained-glass windows that caught and reflected the sun in brilliant colors.

She parked in front and took a minute to glance up at the mansion. It could have been transported from some

European principality. A fan-shaped terrace led up shallow steps to the imposing arched entrance over which was a carved stone shield and coat of arms.

Taking a deep, steadying breath, Elyn got out of the car and dragged her large artist's portfolio from behind the driver's seat.

Ronnie had emphasized how important getting this job would be. "Hundreds of people attend these concerts. Everyone sees the posters and programs, takes them home with them. And there your design will be. It could open all kinds of doors for you. You could get so much work, you'd have to turn some down. People in the Valley really admire creativity, and they like to support local artists. If Regina Conti chooses your design for the concert series, you're in."

In spite of all these reassurances Elyn's heart was pounding as she went up the steps. She had chosen her outfit for today carefully. She wanted to look professional yet with a flair, which was why she'd selected the natural raw silk jacket and a long skirt of dark-blue background scattered with a pattern of muted fall leaves.

As ready as she would ever be, she pulled the leather thong of a mission-type bell beside the massive oak door. As she waited for the door to open, she heard from close by the thunk of tennis balls being volleyed. Curious as to the direction the sound came from, she looked around. Above a hedge of huge, blooming blue hydrangea bushes she saw the top of a wire fence, behind which must be the tennis court. She heard voices and laughter. While she was still waiting for someone to answer the door, a man in a white T-shirt and shorts carrying a racquet ran onto the terrace. When he saw her, he stopped, shook back curly dark hair from his forehead and smiled broadly. "Well, hi there!"

Dr. Vin Conti! In tennis whites he was twice as handsome as he'd been in green scrubs in the ER. Smiling, he asked, "How is Danny?"

"Fine, thank you. He's doing just fine."

"Good." He came closer, then said, "I'm curious. What are you doing here?"

"I have an appointment with your mother."

"With my mother?" He frowned. "What do you do?"

Elyn hesitated then said, "I'm an artist. I've come to present my proposals for the summer concert series."

"I see." He threw back his head and laughed. "I thought at first you might be a masseuse or hairdresser. Mother sometimes has people come to the house to do that." He paused. "So you're presenting your work to Mother. I guess I couldn't sit in on it?"

Elyn felt her face get warm. "That's up to your mother. It *is* a business meeting, not a social one."

"Want me to put in a good word?"

"How could you? You haven't seen my work. That is, unless you have great influence with your mother?"

"Sometimes. Depends. But you're right. She doesn't need my input where this sort of thing is concerned. I was just on my way to shower and change. Maybe I'll just pop in later and take a look.'' He grinned. ''Come on, I'll take you in, anyway.''

He opened the door and led her inside just as an elderly maid was coming down the hallway. ''Oh, Dr. Conti, I was just coming to open the door. Had to put on my cap and apron. Mrs. Conti's expecting company.''

''I know, Serena. This lady is it. Please tell my mother she's here.''

''Yes, Dr. Conti. I'll take her out to the patio where your mother's waiting.''

''Maybe I'll see you later,'' Dr. Conti said. ''And good luck.''

The interview went well. Mrs. Conti, an attractive woman in her early fifties with exquisitely coiffed salt-and-pepper hair, aristocratic features and beautiful dark eyes like her son's, was coolly gracious. Although maintaining a certain dignity, she seemed genuinely impressed by Elyn's drawings. With a few suggested modifications, she chose the one Elyn and Ronnie thought best as well. They then chose the font for the print copy and the headings.

As Elyn rose to leave, Mrs. Conti said, ''We shall have confirmation of which musicians will be performing, and we can send those to the printers as soon as we know for sure.''

Their meeting concluded, Mrs. Conti walked to the hall with Elyn and saw her out, saying, ''I'm sure we'll be in touch, Miss Ross.''

Thrilled at both having her design chosen and the fee

the committee had agreed to pay, Elyn almost floated down the steps back to her car. She was so delightfully distracted, she almost did not see Vin Conti seated in a sleek sports car parked right behind her small economy one.

He tapped his horn lightly and after she stashed her portfolio back in the car, she walked over to him.

"How did it go?"

"Very well. I got the job."

"Great! Congratulations. We should celebrate. How about my taking you to dinner?"

Elyn was tempted. It would be fun to tell Ronnie about. But she was wary of impulsive decisions. More wary still of getting involved with anyone as rich, handsome and powerful as Vin Conti.

"Thanks, but I can't. Danny's with a sitter and I've been gone most of the afternoon. I don't like to be away from him too long."

Dr. Conti seemed genuinely disappointed. "Another time, then?"

Elyn just smiled. Even if Vin Conti asked her out again, she knew she would not accept.

Because of Doug.

It was then that she realized *he* was the person with whom she really wanted to share this triumph.

Chapter Twenty-Three

The Mustard Festival gala was being held at the Francesca Wineries, one of the oldest in the valley and the most picturesque. The old stone building had once been a monastery, and before its present owners—entrepreneurs from San Francisco—monks had lived there and had first produced the world-renowned wine. Instead of Gregorian chant, the music that wafted through the cloisters and out into the evening air was familiar melodies already being danced to by couples in the huge tasting room which had once been the monks' refractory.

Inside, all was light, gaiety, with all the elements of a magical evening. Each of the candlelit rooms presented a new form of entertainment. In one, there were mimes mingling among the guests; in another, trapeze artists performed their acts from the high, beamed ceiling; yet another room was transformed into a French cabaret with round tables covered in red cloths, and waiters dressed in berets and striped shirts. In several of the adjoining rooms sumptuous refreshments of food and wine were being offered as people strolled about.

Just as they entered the formal parlor, someone Ronnie knew called to her and engaged her in an animated conversation while Elyn waited a little apart. She saw Dr. Vin Conti looking splendid in a dinner jacket, a red cummerbund and white pleated shirt. He was standing with his mother. Elyn's glance caught his, and a look of recognition crossed his face. Saying something to his mother, he evidently excused himself and started toward Elyn.

"Hello, there. How nice to see you. How's that young man of yours?"

"Fine, thank you, no recurrence of any problem."

"Good, glad to hear it." His gaze made a sweeping appraisal of her. "You certainly look fine."

"Thank you. Lots of exercise, I guess. Trotting after an active little boy."

"Could I get you something, a glass of wine?"

"No, thank you, I'm waiting for my friend." Elyn saw Ronnie coming through the crowd. "Here she comes now. Veronica Bailey. Do you know her?"

Dr. Conti smiled. "Of course, everyone in the valley knows about The Crow's Nest." Just then, Ronnie finished her conversation and joined them. At almost the same time a familiar voice said, "Evening, Elyn."

"Why, Doug, I didn't know you were coming."

"A last-minute decision. I'm with some clients." He was about to say something more when an attractive brunette came up to him and slipped her hand through Doug's arm. "We've got a table and we're waiting for you, Doug."

Elyn felt a small jab of surprise, or was it something else? Somehow she had not thought of Doug as having a social life. But she didn't have time to think about it because Ronnie was tugging her arm, saying, "Looks like you have two interested parties. Doug, of course, and Vin Conti."

"No way, Ronnie. Dr. Conti was only being polite. He wanted to know how Danny was. And Doug was just—"

"You are so naive, Elyn. Don't you know how glamorous you look tonight in that outfit?"

This year's theme was the Gay Nineties. Ronnie had found a royal-blue taffeta dress overlaid with black lace, with leg-o-mutton sleeves and a ruffled bustle to set off Elyn's naturally slender figure. Elyn's hair was swept up under a tiny pancake hat made of blue feathers with a flirtatious black net veil.

"Come on, let's look at some of the exhibits," Ronnie urged, taking her arm. "There are some people I want you to meet. And don't be shy, speak up, talk about yourself, tell them you're the artist doing the Vineyard concerts this summer."

"You should be my agent," murmured Elyn.

Elyn was used to Ronnie's coaching. But, of course, she would never put herself forward like that.

Ronnie was also off track about Vin Conti. His type

of man did not appeal to her in the least. Not after her experience with Dex's high-powered, superficial charm. Doug Stevens was actually more interesting. She found herself curious about his unexpected appearance tonight, and the stunning woman he was with. She realized she had taken him and his friendship rather for granted. Now she knew Doug had a whole other life she knew nothing about.

"Now there's someone you must meet—Olive Hill." Ronnie's whisper brought Elyn back from her speculation about Doug.

"Who is Olive Hill?"

"You don't know? Don't you subscribe to the Valley News? She writes a column 'The Grapevine' and does feature stories, profiles of interesting people. She also reviews plays or exhibits, anything that brings out the city's society people. Everyone reads Olive Hill."

Except me evidently, Elyn thought, as Ronnie guided her through the crowd toward a small, vivacious woman who was chatting to a distinguished-looking bearded man.

When they reached her, Ronnie waited for a chance to speak. Meanwhile, Elyn had the opportunity to study the woman. Olive Hill was short, stocky and animated. Her ink-black hair was cut in straight bangs, then pulled severely back into a bun. Her mouth was a slash of vivid red lipstick in a face almost as whitely powdered as a Japanese geisha. She was holding a wineglass in one hand while she gestured with the other. Finally, Ronnie was able to catch her attention and as soon as her conversation with the gentleman ended, Ronnie gently pushed Elyn forward.

"Miss Hill, it's so nice to see you again," Ronnie said. "We met last year at the Mustard Festival. I'd like you to meet one of the Valley's talented artists, Elyn Ross."

"Hmmm." Olive Hill scrutinized Elyn, then whipped out a notebook from a voluminous shoulder bag. "The artistic quotient here is very high which is what we were just discussing."

"Elyn is the creator of the bestselling greeting cards Sophisticats," Ronnie volunteered. "Also her design has been chosen for the summer vineyard concert series logo."

Miss Hill's eyes darted back to Elyn. "I always like to promote Valley artists. I'd like to do a piece on you. When can I come to your studio? What day do you have free?" Her pen was poised expectantly, ready to jot down a date.

A bit overwhelmed by the woman's quick response, Elyn was momentarily speechless until Ronnie's discreet elbow jab prompted her to reply, "I work at home, so most any date that suits you would be fine. Mornings are best for me when my little boy is at day care."

"Oh, you have children? That makes it even more provocative. Working mothers, especially ones doing creative stuff, are particularly good copy. And is your husband supportive? Or not? Either way makes an interesting angle.''

Luckily, Elyn did not have to answer. Someone drew Olive Hill away to talk to the leader of a mine group. The rest of the evening was fun, the entertainment and food all extravagant. Once in a while Elyn caught sight of Doug. He was still with the same group of people, and they never had a chance to talk again.

After making the rounds of all the booths and exhibits, Ronnie and Elyn watched a spectacular acrobatic show. Later, there would be more dancing in the Great Hall, but Elyn did not want to keep her sitter too late and Ronnie was agreeable to leave.

On the way home Ronnie exclaimed, ''Wasn't connecting with Olive Hill a stroke of good luck?''

''Mmm-hmm,'' Elyn murmured. But it was Doug, not Olive Hill, Elyn was thinking of. In his white dinner jacket he had looked incredibly handsome tonight. If only things were different, maybe... But right now she had to concentrate all her energies on Danny. Make their future safe, secure. Danny would need her even more as he got older. Unconsciously she sighed. A committed relationship—marriage—seemed like a dream she'd had a long time ago. She had made one terrible mistake. She could not afford to make another one.

When they reached Elyn's cottage, Ronnie said, ''Tonight will pay off, believe me. Wait and see if I'm not right.''

Chapter Twenty-Four

Three weeks later, Ronnie's prediction came true. Elyn was sitting at her drawing board, working when she heard the screech of tires outside. Next came Ronnie's voice. "Elyn, what did I tell you? You're famous. Wait till you see this!" She came rushing into the studio, waving a newspaper. "Olive Hill's column in this week's paper."

Elyn gave a little groan. Reading about herself made her very uncomfortable. She grimaced at Ronnie.

"Go on, read it!" Ronnie urged.

"I *am!* That's the trouble," Elyn said and continued to read.

Tucked away in the midst of shadowing oaks is a small cottage where artist Elyn Ross lives and works. You enter through an arched gate, walk up a meandering path bordered with a variety of flowers to a denim-blue door.

Elyn, a slender blonde with shoulder-length hair, wearing a paint-smudged smock, welcomes you with a smile. The first thing you notice about her is her dark-lashed brown eyes, their candor and warmth. She ushers you through the center hall to her studio, once the dining room of a vineyard overseer's house. A drawing table is placed in the alcoved window that looks out across what used to be acres of the Thorne family vineyard and beyond onto the country road.

Elyn's work is getting more and more recognition locally. Her greeting cards known as Sophisticats are gaining national popularity. The suave, worldly theme of these cards seem a complete contrast to the reserved, almost shy personality of their creator. Unwilling to discuss her personal life, Elyn talked openly about her hopes and goals for her art. She told me a little wistfully that she would like to do more painting. "But there's food to be put on the table, shoes to buy every few months for Danny and bills to be paid. I've been fortunate to break into the greeting card market and Sophisticats have been very good to us."

Elyn's life revolves around her son, Danny, a towheaded, bright, unspoiled youngster, who came in the house bringing his puppy as we were winding up our interview. When I asked him what the dog's name was, I was told "Gabe," short for Gabriel. "Because he's like my guardian angel. He looks out for me.''

From what I saw of Elyn Ross's work and learned from talking with her, I see great things in store for this charming young woman who has made a life for herself and her small son in perfect harmony with her artistic career.

Elyn put the paper down with a frown. ''It's almost, well, *too* much.''

''*Too* much? Don't be silly. Olive tends to write purplish prose, but haven't you heard the logic that any publicity is good as long as they spell your name right? Name recognition. Word of mouth. Olive Hill has connections in the art world as well as in the social milieu. Be grateful!''

''Yes, but I hadn't meant to be so open, to talk so much about myself...and my life. I guess I didn't realize she was taking down everything I said. It makes me feel so...*exposed.*''

''I think it makes you sound interesting,'' Ronnie said staunchly. ''Think of it as part of building your career.''

But Elyn wasn't so sure. She had an uneasy feeling her interview with Olive Hill might bring her more than she bargained for.

Elyn didn't have much time to worry about the repercussions from Olive Hill's column. Her life was suddenly very full. There was the upcoming vineyard concerts. Her design required consultations with the printer about reproducing them on posters, brochures and programs.

Then the day the summer series of Vineyard Concerts began, Elyn received the wonderful news that the Mustard Seed line was accepted and would go into production soon.

It was certainly the inspiration she'd prayed for that day at the mineral pool when she'd struggled to find more purpose to what she was doing. A line of inspirational cards was surely confirmation.

At first she wanted to get on the phone and tell everyone, Ronnie and Lark. But then she decided to wait and tell Doug first. He had asked to take her to the first program of the vineyard concert and then to dinner afterward. That would be the perfect time and he was the perfect person with whom to share it.

Elyn was doubly excited as she got ready that evening. She couldn't wait to see how people reacted to her designs on the programs. She had already received good comments from the people on the committee, but she was anxious to get some general feedback.

When Doug saw Elyn that evening, he whistled. "You look smashing. Beautiful, in fact."

She had on a pale-blue crocheted sweater and a long pleated skirt of darker blue. Her hair was swept up in a French twist and suspended from her delicate ears were Victorian-style pendant earrings. Pleased but a little embarrassed by his extravagant compliment, Elyn said, "Flattery will get you anything!"

Doug made a hopeless face. "If only that were true!" They said good-night to Danny and his sitter, Luisa Ramirez, and went out to the car. Tonight, Doug was driving his sporty compact instead of his pickup.

Before turning on the ignition, Doug gazed admiringly at her in the passenger seat, his expression serious. ''In case you don't realize it, Elyn, it's getting harder for me to stick to our bargain. I haven't changed the way I feel about you. I'm still hoping that you will have second thoughts about us. It could be really wonderful—us together.''

''Please, Doug, let's not—''

''Okay. I'm a man of my word. Consider the promise intact.'' He switched on the engine, then frowned. ''I can still say I think you're beautiful, can't I?''

''Yes, and thank you.'' Elyn smiled, relieved that the awkward moment had passed so smoothly.

The Casa Conti was even more spectacular in the evening. There were tiki torches all along the driveway leading up to the house and colorful Japanese lanterns lighted the stone terrace.

It was a perfect evening for this outdoor event. There had been a gorgeous sunset and the sky still held some color but was fading into a mauve-colored dusk. A pencil-thin moon was rising above the old oak tree that surrounded the house and lined either side of the area where the audience would sit. Folding chairs had been placed in semicircular rows. A platform had been constructed in front for the orchestra.

This first concert of the series was the big event of the

summer social season in the Valley. Elegantly dressed women escorted by men in summer evening clothes filed in, a murmur of voices as they chatted with friends and found their seats.

Elyn was thrilled to see all were holding programs with her design on the covers. She hoped they were admiring them, maybe commenting on them. In the lower right hand of the design were her signature initials *LN,* and inside she was given credit: "Designer, Elyn Ross."

There was a stir of anticipation in the audience as the musicians took their places and started tuning their instruments.

Elyn and Doug were escorted to their seats by volunteer ushers. A few rows back, Elyn spotted Ronnie and her new beau, Greg Michaels. Ronnie saw her and waved her program, making a circle with her thumb and forefinger denoting approval.

Soon after the musicians were settled, the conductor walked on stage. Applause broke over the quiet summer evening as he took his place at the podium and rapped his baton on the music stand.

Gradually the lyric beauty of the first selection spun its magic. As it happened, it was a piece Elyn often played on her stereo while she was working. As usual she found herself lifted by the beautiful rendition. The rest of the program was equally satisfying.

Finally the concert came to a close. There were two encores followed by enthusiastic clapping. But then the maestro made a bow and left the stage. There was no calling him back.

Eventually the applause petered out, the audience desisted and stood up. Everyone began to move in small groups toward the terrace where the buffet had been set up. The light from the lanterns shone on the sparkling crystal wineglasses, and the silver platters of delicacies on the tables covered with antique lace cloths.

Elyn searched for Ronnie and her date, but somehow they were lost in the crowd. The crush of people blocked Elyn's view, but suddenly she went cold. For a heart-stopping few seconds she thought she saw Dex. A man moving toward the terrace with a group of people looked like him—the shape of the head, the set of the shoulders in the well-fitting white dinner jacket. But, no, it couldn't be. Not possibly.

The crowd drifted away and she lost sight of the man. But not before she suppressed a kind of sick shudder. She was surprised that even the thought of him would have such an effect on her. Doug touched her arm, bringing her back from a past she did not want to remember.

''Let's skip the reception and grab that dinner I promised you,'' he suggested. ''I'm starving. Good music always makes me ravenous.''

Elyn knew Ronnie would probably think she should stay, mingle, be acknowledged as the creator of the program design, but somehow she felt strangely shaken by that false sighting of Dex. A quiet dinner with Doug where she could share her news about the new Mustard Seed cards was more appealing.

"Let's go," she said.

The Grape Arbor was a newly opened, already popular restaurant in St. Helena. Seated at a corner table, they were approached by a young waiter who rattled off the specialties, then left them to place their orders. Elyn made a quick choice, eager to tell Doug about her new line of cards.

"Elyn, that's wonderful," he said when she shared her news. "I can see this means a great deal to you." He reached across the table and took her hand.

"I want to say thank you for all that you've done for me." Elyn paused and instead of withdrawing her hand, curled her fingers around Doug's. "With friends like you, Doug, I've been able to bring Danny up in a circle of love."

"It's also a confirmation of your own faith, Elyn. I've seen you struggle and I've watched you grow. You have so much depth now. That little shell you formed around you has given way to a warmth, an openness that is, well, truly beautiful to behold."

Doug's eyes moistened a little. Elyn had never seen him so moved. What else he might have said was interrupted by the arrival of their salmon filets. The moment that trembled between them ended.

Elyn realized she hadn't been able to eat since she had received the acceptance letter, and she was now very hungry. They both ate with enjoyment while discussing other aspects of her new line.

When their waiter returned to ask them about dessert, Doug listened to the choices and suggested, "Let's be really decadent and have the cheesecake with red raspberry sauce."

"Okay, let's!" Elyn agreed.

They were just served dessert when something happened, completely wiping out every other thought.

The entrance to the restaurant was in Elyn's direct view. Just as she was about to speak, a group of well-dressed people entered, laughing and talking. Among the couples one person stood out. Elyn's heart dropped. No mistake now. It *was* Dex she had seen at the Conti Vineyard concert. From there he'd come to this new, trendy restaurant. She knew San Franciscans thronged to the summer concerts; she just had never dreamed Dex would be among them.

She watched in frozen disbelief as the group was greeted by the maitre d'. Evidently they had reservations because he led them through the restaurant to the adjoining private dining room.

"Come on, Elyn. You can't chicken out now," Doug teased as he picked up his fork and took a bite of the cheesecake.

Elyn was unable to concentrate. Her mind was fixed on a horrible thought. What if Dex had noticed her name on the list of credits on the program? Dear God, she hoped not. She tried not to think that on the other side of the restaurant was the man who had changed her life forever.

Her head began to pound. Doug glanced at her anxiously. "Something wrong, Elyn?"

She stared at him blankly as her mind whirled. How to escape the chance of running into Dex? To avoid the risk, she had to get out of the restaurant. They couldn't linger over coffee.

"Sorry, Doug, I'm afraid I'm getting a headache."

"Have you something to take, an aspirin?"

She shook her head. "I'm sorry, I think we better go."

Doug was immediately solicitous. "Probably all the excitement today. Your good news, then the concert. Come on, we'll leave right away."

When they reached the cottage, Doug waited while Elyn got a report about Danny from the sitter so he could take her home. At the door Doug kissed Elyn lightly. There was no time nor privacy to do anything more.

"Hope you feel better tomorrow," he said.

"Thanks, I'm sure I will." Not sure at all. Not after what had happened.

Elyn stood there, watching the taillights until they disappeared at the end of the road. Maybe she should have confided in Doug, told him about seeing Dex.

It was lonely keeping secrets. Having no one to share this frightening experience with. Elyn leaned against the door frame weakly.

But what good would it have done to tell Doug?

She'd thought she was beyond reacting to thoughts of

Dex. But this was different. He'd been here in the Valley. Would he come again? Was there any chance he might see her?

She came inside and closed the door. Suddenly, she felt tired. She went to check Danny, then gulped down a couple of aspirin and went to bed.

But sleep eluded her. She lay there for hours. Why had seeing Dex been so upsetting? It wasn't that she had any feelings for him anymore. The reminder that he could step back into her life at some time with no warning frightened her.

Suddenly Elyn's thoughts turned to Doug. How lovely it would be to feel the comfort of loving arms around her, to go to sleep tonight with her head on someone's shoulder, to know that he would be there, next to her, when she woke in the morning, ready to share with caring for Danny.

Chapter Twenty-Five

Sunlight streamed through the windows the next morning when Elyn came into the kitchen. Somehow it made the memory of last night's ghosts fade. Or at least not to loom so threateningly.

Dex's being at the concert was happenstance, she told herself. People came down to the Valley from the city all the time. Did he? Maybe he knew someone with a house where he spent weekends? Was there a chance she could run into him again? Anywhere? Anytime? The thought chilled her. And what would Dex's reaction be if he knew about Danny?

Determinedly Elyn thrust away all these possibilities. She couldn't live in fear. She refused to let the shadow of her past ruin the new life she had made for herself.

She made coffee, and drank two cups standing at the sink, staring out over the hillside. When Danny woke, she fixed his breakfast, walked him down to the end of the road where the St. Luke's van picked him up for day care.

When she got back to the house, the phone was ringing. It was Ronnie.

"How does it feel to be the star of the show? You should have stuck around. Your ears should be burning with all the compliments your design was getting." She halted. "Hello? What's wrong? I'm not getting the reaction I expected."

"Well, something happened last night that spoiled things." Elyn paused, then said, "I saw Dex."

Ronnie gasped. "You *what?*"

"At the concert, then later at the restaurant where Doug and I went to dinner."

"Did he see you?"

"No."

"Does Doug know?"

"No."

"What are you going to do?"

"What can I do? Nothing."

"Well, try not to worry. It might have just been a one-time deal." There was a long silence, then Ronnie said, "Customer coming in, got to go. Sorry. I'll call you later."

Elyn hung up. All the old feelings of anger and betrayal she thought she had overcome rose within her. Knowing that in this frame of mind it would be impossible to sit quietly at her drawing board, Elyn spent the rest of the morning in frenzied activity. She scrubbed the kitchen, polished the cabinets, waxed the floor. At noon, worn-out, she slumped down in the rocker.

A knock at the door gave her a start. When she made her way to the front of the house, she saw Doug at the door.

"Hi, Elyn, may I come in?"

He looked so worried, she could not refuse. He came inside and together they walked to the kitchen.

"You all right?" he asked. "Headache better?"

"Headache?"

"Last night, remember?"

"Oh, yes." She put her hands up, rubbed her temples. "I'm sorry, Doug. I should have explained. The other night—well, truth is, I had a shock."

Doug looked alarmed. "What kind of a shock?"

"I saw Danny's father. First, at the concert, although I wasn't sure it was him. Then later, at the restaurant. There was no mistake. That's why I was so anxious to get out of there. I didn't want him to see us. I'm sorry, Doug. I should have told you."

"I see." Doug said calmly. "How long has it been since you've seen him?"

"Not since I told him I was pregnant."

"That long, huh? Then he doesn't know about Danny?"

Elyn shook her head.

"How did you feel? Seeing him again, I mean?"

"Numb. I don't know."

Doug didn't say anything more for a long moment. "Then he doesn't know you're living here?"

"I'm afraid he may see my design credit on the con-

cert program. If he does—'' her anxiety of that possibility made her voice waver ''—I don't know what will
happen.''

Doug's next question surprised Elyn. ''Do you want
to see him?''

''No! I never wanted to see him again after—no, I
don't want to see him, but I'm afraid.''

''There's nothing to be afraid of, Elyn. He has no
claim on you.''

''That's true, but he does on Danny. Even though he
didn't want me to have the baby, wanted me to have an
abortion, still he *is* the biological father. If he knew about
Danny—'' Her voice broke. ''I've read enough newspaper accounts of fierce custody battles to be afraid.''

''No use borrowing trouble. Maybe you're worrying
unnecessarily, Elyn.''

''I know you're trying to be reassuring, Doug. But you
don't know Dex.'' Elyn hesitated. How much should she
tell Doug about the father of her child? ''If there's anything he feels he has a right to, he goes after it.''

''Look, Elyn, the facts are he didn't see you, has no
way of knowing where you and Danny are. If he's like
a lot of people, he tossed away that program without
giving it a second glance. The chances of his finding you
or knowing about Danny are a thousand to one.'' He
paused. ''Whatever happens, you can count on me to
help—however I can.''

Elyn looked at him. There was so much concern in his

expression. "I know, Doug, and I'm grateful. You're a wonderful friend."

"I'd like to be more than that. If you'd let me." She started to say something, but he held up his hand to stop her. "I know we have an agreement, but deal or no deal, you and Danny are important to me. I can't help it. I love you, Elyn."

Fleetingly Elyn thought how easy it would be to hide in the protecting comfort of Doug's love. But it would be unfair.

"I know."

"Remember. I'm here for you whatever happens."

He leaned down, gave her a quick, hard hug and then was gone.

PART III

Chapter Twenty-Six

Elyn looked up from her drawing table and glanced out the window. Summer was over but the day was sunny and beautiful. Autumn had come to the Valley. The air held the scent of ripening fruit, and the hills were ablaze with vibrant color.

To her immense relief none of her worries had materialized. Dex's attending one of the vineyard concerts and going to dinner at The Grape Arbor must have been a matter of happenstance.

Elyn finished the sketch she'd been working on and signed it with her identifying *LN*. It was one of the new set of designs for her Mustard Seed line which was becoming popular.

She glanced at the clock. Time to pick up Danny from day care. Then she would fix them a picnic lunch to eat outside while the weather was still warm.

When they returned home, she made peanut-butter-and-jelly sandwiches, put some pears and grapes in a plastic bag, filled a thermos with milk and put it all in a basket. Then they carried it out under one of the oak trees.

Elyn had just spread a blanket for them to sit on when a station wagon turned in from the road and drove slowly up to Miss Thorne's house. She saw the sign Valley Realty painted on the side and frowned. She knew Miss Thorne's opinion of the aggressive Leland Parker of Valley Realty. After the tongue-lashing Miss Thorne had reported she gave him on his last try at listing her house, why was he back?

If he thought he could convince Lark to sell her house, acreage and vineyard, no matter how rich a client he had or how much he offered, he was sadly mistaken.

Lark had recently told Elyn, "Nothing will move me from here until they carry me away. I made up my mind about that some time back. I've sold off a few acres, enough to keep me comfortably for a few years longer. But I'm not letting my family's land go to some of these fly-by-nights who want to make a fortune on some development that will ruin this valley. This house has been here for a hundred years or more, and I'm not going to be the one to let it go. Of course, if the right person came along and wanted to reactivate the vineyards... Well, that would be another story."

Ronnie had told Elyn there was a conflict among the people in the Valley about rapid development, the temptation to cash in on the growing popularity of the area, in particular the proliferation of resorts and spas.

But a powerful few were holding out to retain the quality and ambiance that made the area so attractive. So far, this staunch group was winning. They were perfectly agreeable to wealthy tourists coming to spend weekends and their money, but not to change the Valley in any way that would spoil it.

Elyn watched Parker get out of the car as did another man from the passenger side. The assured way the second man moved and surveyed the surroundings was chillingly familiar. Elyn went absolutely rigid. Her worst nightmare was happening before her startled eyes. It was Dex.

As she stood there rooted to the spot, she saw the two men mount the porch steps and stand at the front door. Probably ringing the doorbell. In vain. If she knew Miss Thorne, Elyn guessed she had spotted Parker's station wagon and probably wouldn't answer the door.

Elyn was right. The men turned around and got back in the station wagon. She did not want them to see her as they drove back down, so she hurriedly began gathering up the picnic things.

"Come on, Danny, we're going back inside."

His little face crumpled in disappointment. "But we were going to have a picnic."

"We'll have it inside, now come on."

"I don't wanna have it inside." His bottom lip pushed out in a pout.

Elyn's heart was pounding now. The station wagon was coming down the hill. "Danny, do as I say. Hurry

up.'' Her unusually sharp tone brought tears to his eyes.
She ignored them in her frantic move toward the cottage.
"Come on. *Now.*''

"Mommy, why?''

"Don't argue. Just come.''

Her arms were haphazardly filled with paper plates,
cups and plastic utensils, but things began to spill out,
leaving a trail behind her as she made for the steps.
Danny stooped to help her pick them up. Elyn threw a
panic-stricken glance over her shoulder. It was too late.
Parker's station wagon was pulling into *her* driveway.
Before she could make her escape into the house, he had
parked and was getting out.

"Oh, miss!'' he called. "Could you tell me if Miss
Thorne is away? No one answers up there. I left my card
but...''

Elyn barely heard him. Her eyes were riveted on his
passenger who had also gotten out of the car. In the next
moment she and Dex were staring at each other.

It seemed an eternity. She saw the look of amazement
on his face, the quick recognition. He glanced at Danny,
then darted a quick look back to her. Immobile, she
waited helplessly, but she knew he had made the
connection.

Leland Parker sensed something. He looked from Dex
to Elyn with a puzzled expression. He cleared his throat,
then spoke again. "I'm sorry to intrude, but I wondered
if you knew if Miss Thorne was away? My client—'' he

paused, indicating Dex ''—is interested in this property and...''

Even though the Thorne estate wasn't on the market, Parker held the relentless conviction that enough money would move the immovable object. That was the way Dex's mind worked, too. Money could buy anything. Money could fix anything. Bitterly Elyn remembered the check that had come with the flowers the day after she had told him about the baby. The baby he hadn't wanted, the baby he had wanted aborted. The child he was regarding with such undisguised interest at the moment *was* that baby. Danny.

Elyn heard herself speaking with remarkable coolness. ''No, I don't know if Miss Thorne is in or not. I do, however, know she is not interested in selling her house or land.''

Dex spoke up. ''Parker, this has turned out to be a real coincidence. This young lady and I are old friends. Hello, Elyn, how are you? You're looking wonderful.'' He paused, then smiled at Danny. ''And who is this young fellow?''

''I'm Danny.''

''Well, hello there, young man. Shake hands.'' Dex took a few steps forward and held out his hand. He looked at Elyn. ''Fine little boy, Elyn. How old is he?''

Elyn felt the color flood into her cheeks *You ought to know how old he is, Dex.* Instead, she said nothing. There was no need. Dex had already figured out the truth.

"Uh-huh." Over Danny's head Dex looked at Elyn. "So you live here, Elyn?"

She inclined her head slightly.

"You rent from Miss Thorne then?" Parker interjected. "Then maybe you could tell her we were here." His smile was forced. "And mention that Mr. Sherill is an old friend of yours, that you can vouch for him, and that we'd like to come back and talk to her."

Elyn shook her head. "I can't deliver that message to Miss Thorne. You'll have to contact her yourself."

"I could tell Larkie," Danny piped up.

"No, Danny," Elyn said sharply.

The two men laughed. Dex tousled Danny's hair. "Good boy. But you needn't bother. We'll come back another day and see Miss Thorne." Dex looked at Elyn. "And *you,* Elyn, I'd like to come back and see you. We have a great deal to catch up on. It's been quite a while. Strangely enough, I've been thinking about you lately. I read that piece about you in Olive Hill's column some time ago. Until then, I didn't know you were living here in the Valley. Actually, I had every intention of looking you up once I got settled here." He paused. "You see, I'm very interested in acquiring property here. A vineyard. Building a house. Or at least that was my first intention. That is, until Parker told me about this very desirable property and the lovely old house. He tells me it's been modernized to some extent and could be restored and remodeled—"

"I know it isn't for sale," Elyn said coldly.

Parker interjected, "I haven't contacted Miss Throne in some time. She may change her mind. I think we have a very attractive proposition that Miss Thorne might consider."

Elyn shrugged and turned to go inside the house.

"Elyn." Dex's voice halted her. "I'd like very much to see you. I plan to be here for several days. Could we set a time?"

She felt trapped. Reluctantly she turned and looked at Dex. His expression was determined. She knew there was no way out.

"May I call you?" he said.

"I'm in the phone book." She walked into the cottage, Danny trailing behind her.

Inside, she drew a long, shaky breath. It had happened. The proverbial other shoe had dropped. Her worst fear had happened. The bad dream that had sometimes awakened her in the middle of the night. Dex was back in her life.

Chapter Twenty-Seven

With trembling fingers Elyn dialed Ronnie's shop number. "Dex has been here with Leland Parker looking at Lark's place. He's seen Danny. He insisted that we talk. There was nothing I could do but agree." Almost out of breath, she added, "I'm scared, Ronnie."

"I'll be out as soon as I close up," Ronnie promised.

She arrived promptly at six, bringing tacos from a Mexican take-out place and a chocolate cheesecake from the bakery. Danny was ecstatic, but Elyn found it impossible to eat.

Later, after Danny had been read to and put to bed, the two friends sat opposite each other at the kitchen table.

"I don't know what he's planning. I didn't like the way he looked at Danny. I'm worried because—" Elyn swallowed and put into words the awful fear that had crept into her thinking ever since that morning "—if he actually is planning on buying property and moving to the Valley..."

"Yes, but—"

"Maybe he likes the idea of settling down, owning a place to entertain his San Francisco friends, own a winery. That's just the sort of thing Dex would enjoy. And what better way to complete the picture than a handsome little son?"

"I thought he didn't like kids. Didn't want them in his life."

"That was then, this is now. You should have seen the way he looked at Danny." Elyn tried to suppress a shudder but failed. "Oh, Ronnie, what am I going to do?"

"First of all, you don't know Dex has any such idea. My advice is to wait and cross that bridge when you come to it."

Elyn knew that was good advice. She knew Dex too well to completely rid herself of her fear.

The call Elyn dreaded was not long in coming.

"We have to talk, you know," Dex said after she answered the phone.

"How did you find me...us?" she asked.

"From Olive Hill's column. When I became interested in acquiring property, I subscribed to the Valley News. That's when I learned you were in the valley. I didn't know where exactly. It was only when Parker took me out to the Thorne place and I saw Danny that it all fell into place." He paused for a moment, then continued, "Of course, I had wondered many times where you were." His tone sharpened. "You shouldn't have just walked out without a word, leaving me floundering. How did I know in your state of mind what you might have done?''

She offered no explanation and he went on. ''That wasn't fair, Elyn. You could at least have had the guts to tell me about my son. After all, I have a stake in this, too.''

''I didn't think you wanted any part of him.''

''I was angry. It was a shock. But we can't discuss this over the phone.''

''We don't have anything to discuss. You made that clear when you told me to get rid of our baby.''

''Let's not argue the past. Yesterday didn't just happen. I've been coming to Napa for over a year looking for property, long before I ever saw your name in Olive Hill's column. Yesterday was...what do they call it? Synchronicity? Nothing happens by chance, Elyn. Isn't that what you used to tell me? We have to talk. When can I come out?''

Elyn's hand gripped the phone tighter. She knew Dex well enough to know there was no point in further resistance. She'd have to let him come. And she'd have to be strong. Whatever Dex had in mind, she had to be prepared.

She didn't want Danny to be home when Dex came, so she told him morning would be best. She hoped their meeting would be brief, that he'd be gone before Danny was due home from nursery school. Elyn put down the phone. There was no way out. The encounter she had prayed would never come was about to take place.

The next day, she got Danny off in a robot state. Then she readied herself for Dex's arrival. In the bathroom she put on lipstick, then saw her reflection. The face staring back at her from the mirror horrified her. It was drained of color. The suntan she had acquired through the summer seemed to have faded, leaving her looking sallow and gaunt. Her eyes, dark-ringed from her sleepless night, held fear.

She vacillated between optimism and despair. Maybe the interview would go well. Maybe Dex just wanted to make up financially for the years he had not known about Danny, offer child support. In that case Elyn knew she would take great satisfaction in telling him that was not necessary, that she was well able to provide for Danny, for their needs. She was a successful artist, something he hadn't believed she could become.

At the designated meeting time she saw the sleek new-model Jaguar pull up in the driveway and felt her stomach lurch. She'd been up since five—dreading the movement of the clock hands to this moment.

From the kitchen window she watched Dex get out of the car and come up the porch steps. He looked relaxed, sophisticated, wearing a butter-colored suede sport jacket, blue shirt and gray pants.

She met him at the door. He stepped inside into the front room and glanced in at her studio.

"Have you been doing a lot of painting?"

"Some. My contracts keep me busy," she answered shortly. "Coffee?" She had debated about offering him some, keeping their meeting businesslike. But she knew she needed something to do with her hands.

"That would be nice." He followed her into the kitchen, turned slowly around, surveying the bright-blue cabinets with the fanciful field flowers she had painted on them. "Your work is going well then, I take it?"

"Yes, very. Cream? Sugar?"

"Cream, no sugar, remember?"

She did. But she had wanted to forget everything about Dex. She set out the creamer and sugar bowl, then poured coffee into pottery mugs and placed them at opposite ends of the table.

"I'll get right to the point, Elyn. I've thought about you a great deal, whether you believe it or not. I'm sorry about the way things ended. But they did end. Maybe they would have anyway in spite of what happened. Well, we've both gone on, made different choices, are leading new lives." He stirred the cream in his mug. "You seem reasonably happy, and if Olive Hill is to be believed, you have a thriving career. I'm glad for you, Elyn. That might not have come about if you'd stayed in our relationship. I wanted you available, not devoted to a career. So in the end, maybe it was all for the best."

He seemed to wait for her to comment, but she said nothing. "As I told you, I've been coming to Napa for some time. I want to settle down. I'm planning to invest in property, possibly a vineyard. It's a good investment. I also want to slow down, lead a more leisurely life.'' His mouth lifted in a self-deprecating smile. ''Become a gentleman farmer. Or vintner. So, it seems coming here was not an accident.'' He paused again, took a sip of his coffee. ''Seeing Danny yesterday—seeing *our* child, Elyn—gave me a great deal to think about.'' He put down his mug. ''I realize I want to be part of his life. I have something to offer him now that I didn't have before. I'm going to have a home here in the Valley, probably horses. A little boy would love to have his own pony, don't you think? I could do a lot for a son, Elyn. And that's what I want to do. I hope you agree that it's a wonderful opportunity for all of us.''

Elyn pushed her mug away. Her coffee had grown cold, as cold as her hands felt as she clasped them together. She couldn't believe she'd heard Dex correctly.

''What exactly do you mean?''

''I want joint custody of Danny.''

Joint custody? The words echoed hollowly in her ears, pounded in her brain. He must be crazy.

''You can't.''

''Can't what?''

''Have custody—or anything else. You must be out of your mind to think you can come here at this point and make any sort of demand. You didn't want him before. That settles it for me.'' She stood up. ''Get out! I want you out of here. Don't come back. Ever.''

Slowly Dex got to his feet. ''Don't be irrational, Elyn.

We either have to come to a civilized agreement or fight it out in court. Danny *is* my child. Easily proved with a DNA test. You can't deny that. The biological father has equal rights. Courts today tend to respect parental involvement, however late, in a child's life. Besides, how could I have been involved before since I didn't know Danny existed? That you spirited him away leaving no trace, giving me no option. Kidnapping is a federal offense, Elyn. I believe any judge will rule in my favor, that I've been cheated of my opportunity to be a father to my son.''

''Get out,'' Elyn said again in a choked voice. ''How dare you come here and threaten me.''

''I had hoped you would see reason, Elyn. But since you chose to behave like this, I have only one alternative. We can settle this in court.''

She was shaking so much she could hardly lift her arm, but she managed to point to the door. ''Go...now.''

Dex sauntered to the door and opened it but turned back.

''You know, Elyn, I'm used to winning.''

Elyn had seen that steely look on his face a few other times, though it had never been directed at her before. There was something chilling about that stony glare. There was mockery in it, and something else she didn't want to explore.

She felt an urge to strike that smug expression off his arrogant face. To hurt him, to make him feel the pain he had caused her. She was appalled to realize it would give her immense pleasure to do so. At the same time a prayer sprang up within her. "Help me, Lord."

The tide of anger passed, and she stood, hands clenched into fists, watching him walk out the door, leaving it open behind him. She ran after him, slammed the door and leaned on it with both hands as if to make any thought to return impossible.

When she could breathe again, Elyn went over to her drawing board and slumped down on her high stool. She picked up one of her colored pencils and stared at the last sketch.

Had it been mere days ago that she had sat here, happily rejoicing in her work, her life, waiting to pick up Danny so they could have a picnic outside?

Then in a few minutes everything had changed. Dex had walked casually back into her life. Somehow she couldn't get those happy feelings back.

She remained sitting there, unable to move or to do anything creative, numbed by the confrontation that had just taken place. All at once she became aware of a figure standing in the doorway of the studio. It was Doug.

"Want to talk?"

"No, I want to work." She turned away, feeling her throat tighten.

"It might help to talk to someone. I'm actually a pretty good listener."

"Talking won't solve anything."

"Maybe not, but it can't hurt to try."

She looked at him. All her dormant feelings for Doug

rushed up within her. He was so totally good, a man of integrity, character and faith. She wanted so much to pour out all her fears, her doubts, her anger. But it wouldn't be fair to drag him into this mess that she had brought on herself. Still, there was so much kindness and concern in his face.

"He came out here, didn't he?"

"Yes, he came. It was awful." Her emotion could not be forced back. Her voice broke as she said, "He wants to take Danny." Hot, stinging tears came rushing into her eyes.

"We won't let that happen." Doug's tone was firm.

"He said he'd go to court. He can hire the best San Francisco lawyers. Money doesn't matter to him. I know how ruthless Dex can be in getting something he wants." She sighed. "What chance would I have of retaining full custody of Danny? A struggling artist against a wealthy man who could provide him with everything."

"We need to find out what your options are."

"What options?"

"I'm not sure *legally*. However…" He paused, then walked over to Elyn and said gently, "Marry me, Elyn. No judge in this county, or even in San Francisco would decide to take a child out of a loving home with *two* parents and give him to a man who didn't even want him to be born."

"Oh, Doug, I couldn't do that."

"Why not?"

She shook her head. "It wouldn't be right. Marriage

is sacred. And I know you feel the same way. I've read the words of the ritual in the Episcopal prayer book at Lark's church. It's not to be entered into for convenience."

"You know I love you, Elyn. I have for ages. You and Danny mean the world to me."

"I know, and I am so grateful to you. You are a wonderful friend, but I couldn't take advantage of that. I don't know what I'd do without you."

"You won't ever have to do without me, Elyn. Just say the word."

Doug put his hands on her shoulders and looked down at her, searching her eyes. She leaned against him with a shuddering sigh. She could not keep the sobs from coming. He held her close, saying over and over, "It's going to be okay, Elyn. I promise."

She could feel the strength of his arms holding her. If she could only give way entirely, let him take over, accept all that was implied in what he said. But she couldn't do that.

Even now she knew he was respecting the line she had drawn for their relationship, unwilling to cross it unless she gave permission.

Ironic, that she knew Doug was everything she would need to face what might be ahead of her. Doug was everything she would want for Danny. He would be the perfect solution to her dilemma. But now it would be so opportunistic. So selfish, so unfair. Slowly, she drew away, out of Doug's arms. Reluctantly he released her.

"I have a friend, a very good lawyer. I'll talk to him tonight. See what he advises. Whatever you need to fight this, I'll see that you have it."

"Thank you, Doug. I knew I could count on you."

That night after Elyn did the dishes, wiped off the counters, she left the kitchen and went back into Danny's room. He was lying on his stomach, legs spread out, one arm hugging his Pooh bear, the other holding on to the edge of the blanket which was only half over him. She leaned down to smooth and straighten it, then stood for a few minutes looking down at him.

She felt that sweeping tenderness she had felt in the hospital the first time she had held him. It had been a complete surrendering of herself, a sacred promise that she would make up to him for everything—especially the circumstances of his birth.

At other times through his young life she had been filled with love, affection, caring, but nothing so intense. That sensation had come only during his delivery and now. Something inside her bonded with this child. Something else strengthened within, something powerful, the determination that she was not going to share him with Dex, no matter what.

Long after Doug had left, Elyn lay wide awake. Worn out as she was, still she prayed. Oh, Lord, show me what I should do!

Of course, what Doug had suggested was the solution to her dilemma. But that would be wrong. She knew

Doug had a strong faith. Not that he talked about it, but it was obvious in everything he did. He had the qualities Paul talked about in Galatians 5:22. The fruits of the Spirit. Kindness, goodness, faithfulness, gentleness, self-control. She respected Doug too much. She wouldn't dishonor their friendship by marrying him to save her son.

Chapter Twenty-Eight

Elyn was alone in the kitchen, having her second cup of coffee, when a loud, authoritative knock on the front door startled her. Who could that be? She glanced at the clock. Ronnie? No, too early. It might be an express mail delivery from her editor at the greeting card company. She tightened the belt of her bathrobe and went to answer it.

When she opened the door, a woman she had never seen before stood there. "Elyn Ross?"

"Yes, I'm Elyn Ross. Want me to sign for something?"

The woman did not answer, just pulled out an envelope and thrust it at Elyn who took it. The woman ran back down the porch steps, got into her car and raced down the driveway, leaving Elyn speechless, staring after her.

Elyn went inside and opened the envelope. It was a subpoena. Her hands began to shake as she read rapidly down the page. She was summoned to a court hearing concerning a custody suit filed by Dexter Sherill. The gist of the summons was that at such time, under oath, she would have to answer his charges that she had willfully and deliberately concealed the birth and subsequent whereabouts of his minor child, Daniel, for whom Dex was the plaintiff for equal custody.

Elyn made her way back into the kitchen and sat down. Her knees felt weak and her heart pumped wildly. So that was the way Dex had decided to go. A legal battle that he felt he could win.

Would such a suit stand up in court? A man who had shown no interest before now, claiming she had deprived him of his rights, his fatherhood. What a joke. A sick joke.

But it was serious. She would have to get a lawyer. She would have to call Doug, arrange to see his friend. She hoped he was as good as Doug said. He would have to be because she knew Dex would hire the best.

She needed help. There was so much at stake. Everything. Her life and Danny's. She put her fingers against her now throbbing temples. Dear God, help.

Again, she thought of Doug's proposal. Would Dex stand a chance if she was married? If Danny was in a stable home with two parents, not even a corrupt judge would rule that a child under five should be removed from it.

Had it come to that? Would she stoop to that? To protect Danny?

What was she thinking? She was grasping at straws because she felt so threatened.

There was only One who could help her. She had to trust that her hard-won faith would see her through. Nothing and no one else. Or was that a sham? How confidently she had looked up appropriate Scripture for her Mustard Seed cards. Seeking appropriate verses for all sorts of occasions, ones she believed would inspire, comfort and encourage. If they didn't work for her, how could it be real for anyone else? Faith, "small as a mustard seed," was all that was necessary. She must trust that would be true for her in her need.

Elyn went about the rest of the day in a kind of miasmic fog. She was so paralyzed by the shock of the subpoena, Dex's plans, that she didn't even consider calling Ronnie. Or Doug. She took Danny to nursery school, picked him up three hours later, and couldn't remember what she'd done in between.

That afternoon she tried to work at her drawing table, but it was impossible. Even some possible one-liners for Sophisticats Ronnie had scribbled, failed to bring even a faint smile.

What was the use of trying? All she could think of was the pending hearing. There was so much she needed to do to prepare for it, yet she seemed trapped in a kind of apathy. She threw down her pencil and went outside. It was time to get the mail. She might as well go get it. Anything for distraction.

She walked down to the mailbox, still weighed down with worry.

In her box, along with the utility and telephone bills, was a bulky manila envelope with the return address of her greeting card publishers. She carried the correspondence back up to the house, stuck the bills in her In box and opened the manila envelope. Inside were envelopes of all shapes and sizes. There was also an explanatory memo from the greeting card company secretary. "A bunch of fan mail for your new line. Enjoy." Elyn began to open and read the letters one by one.

"I've never written to a card company before, but I just couldn't resist telling you how much I like the Mustard Seed line. I was first introduced to them when my mother was in the hospital and she received one from her Secret Pal. It really lifted her spirits. The illustration was lovely and the Scripture verse very appropriate. My mother is recovering now, but we both buy and send these cards. They are perfect for so many people, so many occasions. Thank you and the artist."

Each letter was different, but contained the same message. They were overwhelmingly positive, citing incidents when the writer had either received a card or had been looking for one to send and found the Mustard Seed card to be just right.

Tears began to blur Elyn's eyes as she continued to read her mail. She had asked for a sign and God had been gracious enough to give her one. The idea of the Mustard Seed theme had been a gift, now these letters were a further gift. They bore widely scattered post-marks—Ohio, Indiana, Florida, New York. People from all over the country had been touched, and had touched other lives with this one simple yet profound idea.

God had given her the means to use her talent to provide for herself and Danny and in turn to help others. She had only had a little faith when she started out, but like the mustard plant, it had grown, reached out, spread strong branches where others could find comfort, inspiration, hope.

She put the letters in a folder in her file cabinet under Inspiration. In the days ahead she could always read one or two of them and feel her faith renewed.

That night before she went to bed, Elyn took out her Bible and turned to Psalm 32:8. ''I will instruct you and teach you in the way you should go: I will guide you.''

This would be her constant prayer in the days ahead. She would trust Him with her mustard seed faith.

Chapter Twenty-Nine

The evening before the hearing, Doug came out to the cottage.

"You okay?" he asked Elyn, all concern.

"Yes, if you don't ask for details." She smiled, but her lower lip trembled.

"You sure you don't want me to go with you?"

"No, thanks. You've done enough for me already, Doug. Finding me a lawyer was a tremendous help. Jim Hennessy has been great."

"How about if I pick Danny up at day care tomorrow, take him for a hamburger or something?"

"He'd love that, Doug. Thanks."

"Done." Then he said, "I have a little present for you, Elyn." He held out a tiny gift-wrapped package.

At first, Elyn hesitated. Its size sent up small sparks of alarm...and, oddly, excitement.

Doug met her eyes and grinned. "It's safe for you to open it."

When she opened the lid, she saw a tiny, delicately crafted gold angel holding in its hands a tiny mustard seed.

"We never got to properly celebrate your new Mustard Seed line. When I saw this, I knew you had to have it."

"It's beautiful. Perfect. I'll wear it tomorrow. Thank you, Doug."

The day of the hearing, Elyn was up early. She was far less nervous than she expected to be. Lark had volunteered to write a glowing character reference for Elyn to present to the judge who would be hearing the case. The Thorne family name still carried a great deal of clout in the county and Elyn was grateful. Jim Hennessy had impressed her with his competence, sincerity and reassurance that she had a strong case. Ronnie had lent all kinds of moral support from showing up night after night with deli suppers to insisting on helping Elyn choose exactly the right outfit to wear to court.

Elyn awakened with the same prayer she had prayed night and day for weeks. *Help me, Lord.* Then she had turned to her Bible, which was getting well-worn, to look up a Scripture to sustain her.

To her surprise the Bible opened to II Chronicles, a book in the Old Testament she had not read. At the top of the page in chapter 20, verse 15, she read, "Do not be afraid or dismayed—the battle is not yours but God's.''

Elyn was filled with thankfulness. This was exactly what she needed.

She had just come out of the shower when she smelled the fragrance of freshly brewed coffee. Puzzled, she hurried into the kitchen. Doug was standing at the stove.

''Thought you might want some extra help this morning. How do you want your eggs?''

''I'm too nervous to eat. Coffee will be grand, though.'' Elyn slid onto a kitchen stool. She knew she didn't even have to say thanks. Doug was proving what she'd always known about him.

''How'd you get in?''

He turned around and held up a key.

''I always suspected you had one.''

''Never used it before.'' He grinned. ''Not that I wasn't tempted.''

Elyn sipped her coffee.

Doug took a cinnamon bun out of the microwave and placed it in front of her. ''I picked these up at the bakery. Try one.''

To please him, she nibbled on it.

Doug poured himself a mug of coffee and sat down across from her. ''I'll take Danny to St. Luke's, pick him up and bring him home in case you're longer than you expect to be, okay?''

Elyn felt a lump rise in her throat. She couldn't manage another thank you. But she knew Doug knew how grateful she was for all his support.

After breakfast, she drove into town, praying all the way.

Jim Hennessy met her right inside the courthouse door.

"This will be a very informal hearing. We are meeting in the judge's chambers. Just you, me, Mr. Sherill and his attorney." He glanced at Elyn. "You okay?"

Elyn nodded. She knew she looked pale, and that the tension with which she had lived for the past few weeks must show. But her outer appearance was composed. She had dressed carefully to offset any reference Dex or his lawyer might have used to describe her as an artist, a latter-day "hippie." Ronnie had supervised her choice of a cream knit tunic sweater, pleated skirt, taupe pumps and a matching bag. Her hair was swept back and secured with a tortoiseshell barrette.

"Yes, I'm fine," she told Jim.

Although both Ronnie and Doug had offered to accompany her to the courthouse, Elyn knew this was something she had to do alone. She had been alone throughout all of Danny's existence, before his birth and ever since. Besides, she would not be alone. Over and over she mentally repeated the Scripture verse, Do not be afraid nor dismayed—the battle is not yours but God's.

"Okay, let's go then." Hennessy took her arm and they started up the steps to the upper floor. As they reached the top, they saw Dex and another man heading their way from the other direction.

Elyn checked out Dex's companion. He was the perfect TV model for the role of a big-city lawyer, immaculately groomed, expensively tailored.

For a split second Dex's gaze met Elyn's. She was stunned by the lack of warmth in his eyes, but relieved at how little it intimidated her. She felt a flash of confidence. She was no longer the girl who had been so in awe of Dex Sherill, his sophistication, his aura of success and power. She had a core of strength now she had not had four years ago. She didn't flinch nor look away. The four of them walked toward Judge Lucas's chambers.

Judge Joyce Lucas was a striking woman in her fifties. Iron-gray hair was brushed back from a high-cheekboned face; keen hazel eyes watched from behind wide-rimmed glasses. Her air of dignity and composure was visible as she took her place behind a massive, polished mahogany desk. She took up a sheaf of papers in both hands, seemed to skim over them, turning the pages one by one as if refreshing her memory about the case. She glanced at both Elyn and Jim, then over to Dex and his lawyer.

Elyn swallowed. Her throat felt sore with distress.

She kept her eyes straight ahead. *The battle is not mine... Lord, please help me.*

The Judge cleared her throat, then spoke in a refined voice. "You will receive a written statement of my decision through your attorneys, but I was interested in having you come before me in person so that I could reaffirm my own impressions from the dispositions I have received from both plaintiff and defendant.

"Whenever children and custody are concerned, it is always especially important and helpful to meet the couple to make sure that the rights of both are being considered as well as the welfare of the child."

Judge Lucas again looked directly at each of them.

"This will not be a prolonged session. I have read carefully the briefs your attorneys presented to me stating your declarations.

"From Miss Ross's deposition, Mr. Sherill made no effort to locate or contact her for the past three years. Is that true?"

"It is, Your Honor." Jim spoke for Elyn.

Judge Lucas then said, "To be quite honest, I see no reason to award joint custody of Daniel. It is his mother's sworn testimony that the father demanded she abort this baby when he first learned of the possibility of his birth. That from that time he had no contact with the mother, nor at any time did he make any effort to locate her, or visit the child. In other words, it appears to have been a recent decision on the part of Mr. Sherill.''

This time the judge's gaze rested on Dex.

''It would seem obvious that if joint custody were his desire from the beginning, Mr. Sherill would have taken steps to bring this suit up much sooner.''

Elyn clasped her hands even tighter. That was what she'd hoped the judge would emphasize.

''On the other hand, Miss Ross...''

Elyn held her breath, her hope fading. What was she going to criticize *her* for?

''On the other hand,'' Judge Lucas repeated, referring to the brief, ''Miss Ross has been the sole and principal caretaker of this child from the time of his conception, protecting him and bringing him into the world, alone, without any assistance, moral or financial support from the father. She has provided a secure, loving home for him. He has been surrounded by caring friends, both male and female, and is a healthy, happy boy.

''I see no reason to change Daniel's situation. Bringing in a stranger who claims to be his father at this point would only prove bewildering and disruptive. Therefore, Mr. Sherill's plea for joint custody is refused. If, when the boy reaches the age of eighteen, and with the agreement of his mother, wishes to contact Mr. Sherill and establish any kind of relationship, at that time he is legally of age and has the right to make that contact.''

Judge Lucas peered over the top of her glasses. ''If Mr. Sherill wishes to make any sort of financial contribution to the boy's upbringing or future education plans, and that is agreeable to Miss Ross, that can be negotiated through your attorneys. I hereby further recommend Mr. Sherill make no further attempts at contacting the child or harassing Miss Ross in any kind of communication.

''That is my decision and will be so recorded. This case is now closed.''

Outside the courthouse, Jim Hennessy, smiling broadly, asked Elyn, ''Sure I can't take you somewhere for a victory drink?''

''No thanks, Jim,'' she said, feeling almost shaky with relief. ''I just want to get home and hug Danny. But thanks, and thanks for what you did.''

''I just told the truth. I had no serious doubts the judge would go our way.''

As they stood there on the courthouse steps, a sleek, shiny maroon BMW drove by, Dex and his lawyer on their way back to the city, Elyn supposed. Would Dex change his mind about moving to the Valley now, she wondered. It didn't matter. It was over. At last.

Elyn drove home, her heart filled with relief and gratitude. It seemed too good to be true. *Thank you, thank you,* Elyn just kept saying over and over.

She had gotten through it. The thing she had feared most. It had taken courage she didn't know she had, and what faith she had lacked God had supplied.

A blissful joy verging on hysteria took over. She laughed and cried. Was probably a hazard on the road. Jim Hennessy had asked her if she wanted to celebrate. Now that the first shock had worn off, she did. She would fix a special supper. Spaghetti. Danny's favorite. And a salad for full nutritional value to the meal. She might even make a cake. She smiled, thinking that her cooking skills had improved in spite of Doug's teasing.

Elyn made the turn off the road and into the cottage driveway. She saw Doug's blue pickup and felt the most amazing surge of joy. She was home and Doug was waiting.

If she hadn't recognized it before, the truth hit her now. Doug was waiting for *her*. If she said the word, he would be there in the way he'd always been. Doug, the best friend she had ever had, steadfast, strong, dependable. But more than that. Someone she knew she could trust always, with Danny, with her life.

In the side yard Danny was swinging on the tire swing Doug had fixed for him. He waved and called, "Hi, Mom!" as she got out of the car.

She waved back. "Hi, darling." Then she ran up the porch steps and into the house. Before she could call his name, Doug was there to meet her.

"Doug, I won—*we* won! The Judge settled in our favor."

"Thank God, Elyn."

Doug took a few steps toward her.

Suddenly Elyn couldn't hold back any longer. She began to cry. In a second Doug took her tenderly in his arms, held her against him.

"My brave Elyn." He smoothed her hair as she sobbed. "It's all over now. No need to cry. Darling Elyn, I love you so terribly. Please let me love you, take care of you and Danny, spend the rest of our lives together."

Doug lifted her chin so she had to look up at him.

"Okay, Elyn? Say you will."

She could say it now. Express the love she had been afraid to admit, a love she'd never thought she deserved to claim.

"Yes, Doug. I love you, too," she said, knowing it was true.

Elyn wasn't sure how long they stood there holding each other when she heard the screen door slam followed by small footsteps. Still in each other's arms, Elyn and Doug both turned to smile at Danny.

He looked from one to the other, scrunching up his nose in the funny little way he had. He gave them his endearing lopsided grin. "Hey, what's going on?"

Doug glanced at Elyn and she nodded. Doug leaned

forward and held out his hands to bring Danny into their embrace.

"Hey, fella, we've got something to tell you."

Danny looked excited. "A secret?"

"It won't be for long."

Epilogue

The huge airport terminal in Honolulu was teeming with international travelers. Beautiful, dark-eyed Indian women in colorful saris, men wearing turbans and flowing caftans. People of all kinds, sizes, nationalities in constant motion, moving through the various airline counters and numbered flight gates, checking the arrival and departure bulletins.

From where she sat in the passenger lounge, surrounded by baby equipment, Elyn followed the figures of her husband and little boy making their way across the terminal. Doug, with Danny in tow, had gone to check their luggage through to Kona.

Elyn smiled down at the occupant of the infant carrier on the seat beside her. Christie was sound asleep, oblivious to all the noise, foreign voices, activity swirling around her.

Doug had proved to be as wonderful a father as Elyn

had expected. His experience with Danny had been put to good use when their baby was born. And Danny was a loving big brother.

"What a lucky little girl you are, Christie," Elyn whispered to her daughter. "And just wait till your grandparents see you." Doug's mother had written she couldn't wait to hold her new little granddaughter and had a quilt all ready for her.

The senior Stevens had welcomed and accepted Danny as theirs, too, when Doug and Elyn had spent last Christmas with them as a sort of extended honeymoon. They had shown Elyn so much love, so much 'aloha,' her circle of love had expanded.

Counting her blessings, Elyn felt almost overwhelmed. As she often did, she whispered her frequent and favorite prayer, "Thank You, Lord."

*   *   *   *   *

In January 2000
Steeple Hill's *Love Inspired* ®
brings you

A FAMILY
TO CHERISH
by

Carole Gift Page

*After ten years of marriage, Barbara and
Doug Logan find themselves becoming
virtual strangers after the devastating loss
of their five-year-old daughter. As they deal
with their feelings of guilt and grief, can
they heal their marriage and learn
to love each other again?*

**Don't miss
A FAMILY TO CHERISH
On sale January 2000**

Love Inspired ®

LIAFTC_T5

Take 2 inspirational love stories FREE!

PLUS get a FREE surprise gift!

Special Limited-Time Offer
Mail to Steeple Hill Reader Service™

In U.S.	In Canada
3010 Walden Ave.	P.O. Box 609
P.O. Box 1867	Fort Erie, Ontario
Buffalo, NY 14240-1867	L2A 5X3

YES! Please send me 2 free Love Inspired® novels and my free surprise gift. Then send me 3 brand-new novels every month, which I will receive months before they appear in bookstores. Bill me at the low price of $3.74 each in the U.S. and $3.96 each in Canada, plus 25¢ delivery and applicable sales tax, if any*. That's the complete price and a saving of over 10% off the cover prices—quite a bargain! I understand that accepting the books and gift places me under no obligation ever to buy any books. I can always return a shipment and cancel at any time. Even if I never buy another book from Steeple Hill, the 2 free books and the surprise gift are mine to keep forever.

303 IEN CM6R
103 IEN CM6Q

Name _____ (PLEASE PRINT) _____

Address _____ Apt. No. _____

City _____ State/Prov. _____ Zip/Postal Code _____

* Terms and prices are subject to change without notice. Sales tax applicable in New York. Canadian residents will be charged applicable provincial taxes and GST. All orders subject to approval. Offer limited to one per household.

INTLI-299_T5   ©1998

*In January 2000
Steeple Hill's Love Inspired ®
brings you*

BLACK HILLS BRIDE

by

Deb Kastner

For as long as she could remember Dixie Sullivan
had dreamed of building a Christian retreat in the hills
of South Dakota. And when she hired Erik Wheeler
as her foreman, the shy cowboy seemed like the
answer to her prayers. But Erik's tender guidance
was turning out to be more than she'd hoped for,
and Dixie was beginning to wonder if she'd finally found
the man who would make *all* her dreams come true.

**Be sure to pick up
BLACK HILLS BRIDE
On sale January 2000**

Love Inspired ®

LIBHB_T5

Stee[...]
brand-ne[...]
pop[...]

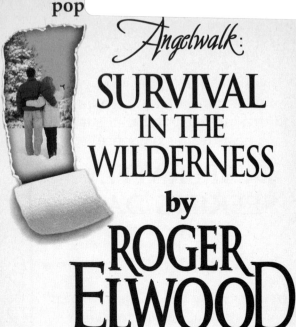

Angelwalk:

SURVIVAL IN THE WILDERNESS

by

ROGER ELWOOD

Louise Currie and her husband, Randy, are on vacation. Everything seems wonderful until their plane crashes and they are forced to survive in the wilderness. They endure cold, injury and hunger as well as find the faith to patch up their rocky marriage. It is that faith in God and in the strength of family that brings this couple closer together.

On sale March 2000 at your favorite retail outlet.

Steeple
Hill™
Visit us at www.steeplehill.com

PLISITW_T5